CONTENTS

Versions of the following stories have appeared in the following places:

Tea and Biscuits first appeared in *Original Prints III* (Polygon)
Night Geometry and the Garscadden Trains first appeared in the *Beloit Fiction Journal*, Vol. 5, No. 1
The Moving House first appeared in *Behind the Lines* (Third Eye Centre)
Genteel Potatoes first appeared in *Bête Noir, 7*
Didacus has appeared in *Stand*, Vol. 29, No. 3 and *The Devil and the Giro* (Canongate)
Sweet Memory Will Die first appeared in *Bête Noir, 6*
The Role Of Notable Silences in Scottish History first appeared in *Bête Noir, 8/9*
Star Dust first appeared in *Streets of Gold* (Mainstream)
Cap O'Rushes first appeared in *New Writing Scotland*, 8 (ASLS)
The Seaside Photographer first appeared in *Edinburgh Review*, 83

Night Geometry
and the Garscadden Trains

A. L. KENNEDY

PHŒNIX

For
E. M. Kennedy
M. Price
J. H. Price
with my love

A PHŒNIX PAPERBACK

First published in Great Britain by Polygon in 1990
This paperback edition published in 1993 by Phoenix,
a division of Orion Books Ltd,
Orion House, 5 Upper St Martin's Lane,
London WC2H 9EA

Copyright © A. L. Kennedy, 1990

Second impression 1994

A CIP catalogue record for this book is available from the
British Library

ISBN 1 85799 066 8

Printed and bound in Great Britain by
The Guernsey Press Co. Ltd, Guernsey, Channel Islands

Tea and biscuits

I went to visit him, late because I had to drive slowly, but I ran all the stairs to make up. He opened the door and I'll tell you what we said.

'You smell the kettle boiling?'

'That's right.'

'Well, do come in.'

'Thank you. Thanks a lot.'

The flat was very like him; in his colours, with his books, his jacket on a chair in the living room. I recognised that. It was warm in there. He must have been home for a while, sitting near the fire with the paper perhaps, and the sleeves of his shirt rolled up.

'Come and talk to me, then.'

'Hn?'

'I'll show my kitchen to you. Come on.'

I was wearing stockings. I like them, because they feel good, but I thought that he would like them, too. I didn't imagine he would see them, or that he would know I had them on, but I thought that he would like them if he did.

Nothing in his kitchen had names on, not even the coffee

1

and tea. Some of it was in jars that you could see through, but for the rest, you would have to remember where everything was. There were ones that he always forgot: rice and porridge, oats and macaroni. I didn't know that then.

When Michael made us coffee he almost gave me sugar as if he expected I'd take it because he did. In the same way, later, I would see him pick up a book and feel it was strange when he didn't put glasses on.

I noticed, back in the living room, when he bent to turn down the fire, that the grey by his temples had faded to white. The cherry light from the gas shone round his head and the hairs that would be pale in daylight showed more red. He was no nearer balding than I remembered – hardly even thin – but his colours were changed, now. I saw that.

My grandfather was in hospital once, a long time ago. Very ill, and though nobody said so, I think he'd had a heart attack. I was taken to visit, just Gran and me, and I saw a stranger in his bed. He wore new, stripey cotton pyjamas. They were something from home and didn't suit the sheets. His head was low in the pillows and I could see his throat, soft and loose where he swallowed. Out of his shirt and pullover he wasn't like my grandfather at all. He was like anyone. Just a man lying down.

I kissed him goodbye and it felt like kissing a man. It felt funny, like when you think of Jesus or a minister being a man. It was like that. I felt guilty. I was seeing him in the way a stranger would. I was seeing his illness. I sat and looked at the bedspread and wasn't nice to him and left, knowing I'd let us both down.

I thought that in the morning our waking would be something like that. Between Michael and me. I thought that I would turn and look at him and see I had wasted it all, that an ageing man I'd once admired would be sleeping, maybe snoring at my side. He would smell of old sweat. I would see that the muscles in his arms were beginning to sink and be frightened by an old face, older in sleep. Slack.

I was wrong; selfish too. Probably selfish.

The warmth of his stomach was fitted against my back and his legs behind my legs were nice, just right. Perhaps his movement had disturbed me, I don't know, but however it happened, it was easy and that was me awake. I answered him with a voice I hadn't heard before, my thoughts running on and feeling new, and as I turned for his arm, I didn't doubt that I could look at him safely and find good. Something good would be there. I wanted him to see as much in me.

He kissed me, I think on the nose, and said 'Good morning.'

'Come here. I want to tell you. I love you.'

'That's nice.'

There are different and better ways to say it. Anything I've ever thought of has seemed to be second hand; something you might have stolen from Tammy Wynette. I should have said that when he ran, and he often did, he ran like nobody else and I loved him for that. He had a rhythm and blues kind of run. Pale socks. I should have said I loved him for every time, but most of all for my first, because he made it a gift and a thing to remember and he was sweet.

That morning was strange. We sat up in bed, recovering slowly, and looked at it and declared it all to be extremely odd. Herring gulls heading to sea again, flying soft and heavy up the street and a light behind the paper shop window, but no sound. The street lamps whispered out below us and the last of the night wore away while Michael brought me tea in bed as if I was somehow fragile after the night.

'How are you feeling?'

'Very nice.'

'You don't hurt?'

'No. I ache a bit.'

'Where?'

3

'You want me to show you?'

'I'm going to have trouble with you.'

I told him that I'd missed the Sixties, and I felt I had a lot to make up. All that permissiveness.

'You missed nothing. Move over, I'm getting cold.'

Perhaps what surprised us both was our luck. When I was still his student we could have tried it, had the affair, plenty of other people always did. There were even two or three times when it could have started, like when my father died and Michael was so nice. He told me that it wouldn't get better, but I could manage it a day at a time. He could have been more sympathetic and tried to get more in return. We could have let it happen then and lasted a couple of terms, maybe more. Meeting again, later, I could have been married, or he might not have been divorced, or something very small could have happened. The day we had coffee together one of us might have been nursing a cold, or depressed and the chance would have gone. Instead we had been lucky.

All through the fogs and the drizzle, until the air became firmer and the marigolds abandoned at the close mouth were feathered every morning with white, all through it, we learned about us. I remembered how new Michael could be. I would catch him, sometimes, smiling in a different light, or say goodbye to him and see him walk away and I would know there were things about him I hadn't begun to find out about yet. That pleased me.

Most of his past I knew, but I couldn't share. Some of the women I might have recognised in the street; certainly, if we'd had the chance to speak. I would have known the perfume, the way they liked to dress and, if they told me stories, I would have heard most of them before. There might be a new one, about this man with brown eyes and long hands who liked to keep chocolate in the fridge. At the end they would call him a bastard and look beyond my shoulder with a tired, short smile.

That was how I imagined it would be. I never had the chance to try. I never met his wife. His ex-wife. Although I wanted to. I wanted to see if she was like him in ways that I was; to see

4

what they had left of each other, and perhaps what would happen to us. Just to set my mind at rest. I told him it might be alright. He said I was perverse, so there you go.

My past was easy. Very short. School: my school friends still in touch enough to have a drink at Christmas, or other times a coffee, if we met. Summer holidays and birthdays and fat-kneed boys in kilts at dances and, almost in spite of everything, no sex. Michael was surprised at that. Sometimes pleased and sometimes guilty, but always surprised at that. The university bit he knew, because he was there and because, like a few of the others, he took an interest in the people he taught. It hadn't been so long, he would tell us, since he was one of us. I had five years to fill him in on: unemployed, then selling insurance, melting down new candles for the MSC and then getting the job. It took me ten minutes to tell him. The picture of me as a baby on the lopsided rug, the yellow-haired, dead father and the mother, he knew all of that.

We announced ourselves to mother, later. Like this.

It happened in the daft days. The New Year was over and the holiday nearly done, a yellow oil of lamplight over the rainy streets. We should have arrived in the summer with light clothes and smiles. Instead our faces were numb and raw, our fingers blind with the cold. We needed to have her tea, to be comfortable by her fire, on the sofa and Father's chair. By the time we had our wits about us, mother was ready.

'Go and fill the pot will you, darling.'

And away I went. I got back and she was interviewing Michael.

It wasn't that we hadn't expected it. It was a natural thing for her to do, but I wish that I could have said something when it happened. Something right. Instead I stood in the doorway, hardly listening, and thought of a book I'd found in Michael's flat. It was a hardback – Persian Art – I don't remember. And when I picked it out of the armchair to put it away I noticed a name and address and a date on the blank leaf at the front. It told me he had lived in a different city, in a house I didn't know and he had bought himself a book, priced in shillings when I was three years old. The nearest I can get to how I felt was how sad it was that he would die before me. How lonely I would be. I don't think, in her interview, mother ever mentioned that.

5

By the way, we hurt her. Not because of what we did, but because I hadn't told her. She hadn't known for all that time. I still saw her quite often with Michael and alone, but always she would speak to me as if I was a guest. She didn't trust herself to me; neither thought nor dream, and every time I saw her, she made me ashamed.

It was almost as if she had died and, perhaps because I had lost her or perhaps because of Mike, or both, I found that I wanted a child. I wanted to make it and have it, for it to be alive with the two of us.

My mother's pregnancy had ended very happily, laughing, in fact. Mother had been watching a new Woody Allen film, I suppose I could find out which one, and suddenly, in a silence, she laughed. She laughed and found she couldn't stop laughing. Her laughing made her laugh. The worry in the face of my father, the little crowd of usherettes, the rush of figures who took her from the back of the cinema to the ambulance; they all made her laugh.

She gave birth within the hour, one month early, still weeping and giggling, amazed, and thinking of that first, secret thing that started her laugh.

I was not born even smiling, only a little underweight.

I wanted a child. I wanted it born laughing, they wouldn't be allowed to make it cry. I would tell them and Mike would make sure. I would have asked him to. It would have been good.

Before the end, before I start on that, there are too many things that were good that I remember. Sitting here, the rungs of the bench are against my spine and a crowd of sparrows is rocking a holly tree, but, behind them, it is quiet. Very quiet. There is space.

I always seem to think of Michael in the kitchen. He is at his clearest then, perhaps because we were busy together there, visiting each other, interrupting, letting things boil. I can smell the wet earth from the potatoes, our red, clay soil. He takes oranges and orange scent from a brown paper bag.

'Fifty pence for five. That's not bad. They're big.'

'You're mean, you know that? I've noticed.'

'They're big oranges, look. I'm not mean.'

'You're stingy.'

'Nice, cheap oranges. I am not stingy.'

'You're a stingy, grouchy, old man.'

He was wearing the big coat, the blue one. It smelt of evening weather and the car. I slipped my arms inside it and around his waist. That was something I did a lot.

'You're just after my oranges.'

'That's right.'

Michael stood very still for a while. He said,

'You do make me happy sometimes. You don't know.'

The dinner was good, with oranges after.

If I'd come to the park last week the afternoon would have been longer, but evenings come in fast now. You can see the change from day to day. By the time I get home the lights will be in the windows and Michael will be back, the fires on. He doesn't like the house to be cold.

I will tell him then. I think I will tell him.

I went there because it's a public service. In the student days we came for the tea and biscuits, but it felt good afterwards, just the same. You knew you could have saved a life. You hadn't run into a burning building or pulled a child out of the sea, but part of you had been taken and it would help someone. I liked it when they laid you on your bed with so many other people, all on their beds, all together with something slightly nervous and peaceful in the air.

They would talk to you and find a vein, do it all so gently, and I would ask for the bag to hold as it filled. The nurse would rest it on my stomach and I would feel the weight in it growing and the strange warmth. It was a lovely colour, too. A rich, rich red. I told my mother about it and she laughed.

I gave them my blood a couple of times after that, then my periods made me anaemic and then I forgot. I don't know what made me go back to start again.

Nothing much had changed, only the form at the beginning which was different and longer and I lay on a bed in a bus near the shopping centre, not in a thin, wooden hall.

Afterwards they send you a certificate. It comes in the post and you get a little book to save them in, like co-op stamps. This time they sent me a letter instead. It was a kind, frightening letter which said I should come and see someone; there might be something wrong with my blood.

I am full of blood. My heart is there for moving blood. The pink under my fingernails is blood. I can't take it away.

And now I am not what I thought I was. I am waiting to happen. I have a clock now, they told me that. A drunk who no longer drinks is sober, but he has a clock because every new day might be the day that he slips. His past becomes his achievement, not his future. I have a clock like that. I look at my life backwards and all of it's winding down. I think that is how it will stay. I think that's it.

Should I say it to Michael like that? Should I tell him that thing I remember about the American tribe. Those Indians. They thought that we went through life on a river, all facing the stern of the boat and we only ever looked ahead in dreams. That's what I'll have to do now.

I think he told me about that. It sounds like him. It would give us some kind of start for the conversation.

Translations

The dog with the broken paw was barking again. Three days it had lasted, the children in the street trying to feed it and stone it alternately, and he wondered now if perhaps it would live after all. And fade back into the mass of dusty or muddy street dogs and be just a little more crippled than the rest. He was glad he hadn't killed it when he saw it first. He killed too many things.

He looked back at the girl, asleep now, and filling the hut with the smell of girl sweat. When it was dark she would go and that would be it finished. Again.

He had already buried her baby. Deep and tightly wrapped where the dogs wouldn't dig. The girl moved slightly in the blankets, her face soft with the possibilities of sleep. He looked at her and smiled.

'This shall ye have of mine hand: ye shall lie down in sorrow.'

He smiled and shook his head and the smile went away.

'Tch. Tch. Tch.'

Staring at the wall beside her, the flattened petrol cans and plastic sheet, he began to whisper, to push himself into her dreams. He began to tell her how the magic that had killed her daughter first came to him. His gift with the dead. His story.

It was time for them to come south again to the clearing by the yellow rivers where the corn would be tall and ready for them to cut. A few more days and the jungle would choke it, it would rot.

He had followed the path they all followed, heard the tiny sounds of their breath and feet, always smelling for tapir, for deer to kill, and yet something of him was not with them. It held back.

And then, when he slept, an aguardiente burn in his throat from drinking the harvest in, his mother came to his hammock and took him away. His dead mother, although she seemed quite well, came and took his spirit and walked it in amongst the other dead. Like a child again, he moved unsteadily for fear of falling and anything he saw, he named to make it safe. Naturally there were things without names and things he couldn't recognise, but he kept within reach of his mother and she could make them stay away.

That was the way it was in the beginning.

A jungle cat, a big one, passed him, close enough to feel its sour breath and its heat in the night. He couldn't see it, of course, because it was living and he was, temporarily, dead. His mother imagined them up into the branches of great trees and, from there, he could guess the progress of many cats as they peeled the souls from other creatures to eat their flesh. Coatuse, anteater, monkey, pig; they appeared in the dark, like blood; here a pinprick, there a scratch and then a flowering gash before a solid mass congealed and ran, or hopped, or fluttered towards the forest of the dead. He couldn't go there. Once you were in you couldn't get back.

Next morning the steam rose from the black soil patches they had cleared and he woke to remember how much he had missed his mother. He remembered her smell and it was on him, as if she had come and held him in the night. He knew this would be the last corn he harvested. He would move towards the east again when everyone started off, but he would leave them before they reached home and go to find the One Handed Man. The One Handed Man would give him cat's blood to drink and tell him what his mother's visit meant. He would be told if it was destined that he should have magic given him and perhaps, one day, replace the One Handed Man. Perhaps something else.

His poison gourd, his darts and his pipe were duly given up.

His father held them strangely, as if they were precious and frightening, as if they already belonged to someone dead. A wife gone with the fever and a son who would follow her, alive; his father seemed somehow bewildered, shorter and beginning to be old. He walked softly in the mud of the path while his eldest boy started to move in the pathless green and brown of the jungle which would take him away and make him a stranger.

Each night, the family would leave a little food for him now, so his spirit would not trouble them and they would glance at the air above their offering with love. They would sometimes smile.

The journey to the One Handed Man was never certain. The way was always changing, like water, and for some it could last for days while others would say they had come to him almost at once. No food could be eaten and no blood shed until the journey's end and he had walked on without his weapons, unable to hunt or defend himself and so in the necessary state of grace. It was possible he would be killed on the journey, or that he would starve. This was also necessary.

When he slept that night he travelled no further than his dreams. Behind him, in the forest, a pale bud opened for the first and only time and let its unrepeatable scent rise to the moon.

The smell of cooking corn meal woke him and, when he opened his eyes, the One Handed Man, his hut and his fire were ready and waiting. The hut wall was casting a shadow across his feet.

'You want to know how my hand was lost, don't you, young man?'

'No. No, I don't.'

'So they've told you already. What have they told you, young man?'

'You were fighting with a spirit. A great, old spirit. I don't remember which. And you wrestled with him for month after month. You wouldn't let him go. In the end he had to bite off your hand before he could run away.'

'Uh hu. Do you want to know the truth?'

11

'Yes.'

'Really?'

'Yes. If I can understand.'

'I lost my hand when I was your age, fishing with dynamite. I was showing off; lighting the sticks and holding on to them, not throwing them into the river, straight away. Do you believe I have magic?'

He was surprised when he couldn't say yes.

'Do you?'

'I. Yes.'

The One Handed Man struck him with the flat of his machete. It was so sudden, it took a while to hurt.

'Only believe I have magic when I prove it. Do you understand that?'

'I think so.'

'You'd better do more than think. More and more people will tell you they have magic. Magic like the sticks of dynamite. Don't believe them. Will you promise me that?'

'Yes.'

'Mh hm. Mh hm. I'm going to give you a drink now. Have you eaten on the journey?'

'No!'

'Good. You can drink this, then. Be careful, it's bitter, but drink it all.'

He drank what he was given and, almost at once, he knew he would fall asleep.

Insects drawn to the firelight stumbled against his face as he came to himself again. It was entirely dark. How many times it might have been dark since he slept, he didn't know.

'Young man? Young man.'

The voice so close, he could feel the words.

'Something will happen now. Are you ready?'

He turned where he lay, finding himself in blankets in the corner of a long, almost empty hut. There were dark things hanging from the roof.

'No, lie on your side. Face towards the doorway and look at the fire.'

He felt the One Handed Man step across him and he did as

12

he was told. When the blanket was lifted away from his back, he shivered and then he felt the pleasant cold, the following warmth of another body, closing tight against his waist while the blanket was folded round again to cover them both.

'You won't be afraid of this, will you, young man? Because this is not a frightening thing.'

When he was old – older than his father had been when he died – he still dreamed of the One Handed Man and the nights in his hut. He would wake and remember the hand and the ointment, pushing between his legs, sliding and hot, the other arm around his stomach, gripping, and the ugly pressure of the stump against his thigh. He remembered when he was no longer in possession of himself, when he was an empty thing.

Most of all he would remember how much he believed it was magic that was pumping into him.

'Ah, young man.'

The lines of morning sun were already sharp through the walls of the hut. The doorway was bright. He was usually left alone now, left to sleep, but there was breath still damp on his cheek today and a hand, sticky with ointment, stroked his chest.

'Mh mh. Now you must ask me what you came to find out. Or you could stay here with me, which you don't want to do. You don't want that? So why did you come?'

'I had a dream.'

'Of course you had a dream. You're too young to have a sickness, so you must have had a dream. Dreams and sickness are all your kind ever come with. Which dream?'

'My mother took my spirit away to walk with the dead.'

'And your mother's dead?'

'Yes.'

'How long?'

'Since I was small.'

'Since you were small.'

He smiled, but it wasn't a laughing smile.

'Since you were small. What else?'

'I saw many animals – '

'What else did you have to ask?'

'I had nothing.'

13

A finger traced round his shoulder.

'What else?'

'I. When I had the dream. I thought it might mean...I thought I might have magic. I would get it. I thought I might be like you.'

'Young man. Not too like me, hmm?'

'But can I? Have magic? Have you been? Do I have it now?'

'You had it before you came. Since you were small.'

That smile again.

'Oh, smile young man, you can believe me. I will show you your magic and I will let you believe in mine. Will that please you? Will that be good? Tonight you will sleep alone and I will take your spirit away and show it magical things to please you. Satisfied? But now you'll have to please me and take this little spirit of mine away.'

Afterwards he sat against the wall of the long, empty hut with a blanket round his shoulders and he cried. He cried until he was hurt and empty and on until he forgot he was crying at all. The sun set and he was crying, shaking with chill and crying and unable to sleep on his own.

He thought about going home and knew he would be different, so that would be different, too. That was how it would be, he knew. He had imagined the bravery of this part – himself, preparing himself to be brave, to see magic. Then the return to the village and being outside and above it, because it was less than small. It was like his own death and it made him angry because it was such a careless death. The pain of it expanded, sick and numb.

'Young man. Young man. Come with me. Come on.'

Arms around him, almost his mother's, but the smell of the One Handed Man.

'Where?'

'Nowhere; you're going nowhere. Turn around.'

He saw himself sleeping, curled into his stomach, and the blanket across his face. He didn't move in his sleep.

'No. You're only dreaming; a still dream. And you'll stay here, sleeping, and you'll come with me, because this is magic, isn't it? Tell me this, now, can you fly?'

'No.'

'Tch. Tch. Tch.'

And so he flew, among the ripe, basking dead, and among the spirits and the little gods and then beyond even them. He flew between magic and colours. It felt like love.

The dog had fallen into silence; he couldn't be sure for how long, or perhaps it was still barking, only too far away to hear. He realised his arms were outstretched, that he was smiling. The things a man does when he thinks of his very first love. He was smiling again.

Because all that time ago, surrounded by leaves and pillars of impossible, rushing light, he fell asleep. Supported by nothing more than the grip of the One Handed Man around his wrist he had lain back on nothing and dreamed. Beautiful.

He saw the impossible light fall and run along corn leaves and warm the earth and he lay on his back under nothing but clear sky, not even a branch between him and so much blue, made of so many blues. If he narrowed his eyes he couldn't see the clearing's edge, just sky.

'What are you doing there, are you sleeping? You'll be sleeping with a snake, if you're not careful. The pig killed most of them, but one left behind is enough. Stir yourself. You'll fry yourself out here, Andrew. Up you get.'

The Fathermacdonalt. He gave everyone names: Andrew, Jonah, Cain. It made him happy and they took care to remember, when he spoke to them, which name belonged to who. He spoke to them most of all about his God: the god of lost children. Having no children of his own it seemed to please him to make children of them all and to adopt them on behalf of his lonely god. They liked him. He spoke their language well, almost too beautifully, and what he didn't know of their ways, he learned. He also knew a great variety of songs. Still, they had all been glad when he asked them to help him to build his house a little away from them, in a clearing of its own.

Andrew smiled at the Fathermacdonalt.

'Amen.'

'Amen, indeed, Andrew, and praise the Lord, but are you feeling well? You're cold as the clay. Come on inside and we'll see if we can warm you. You're back from your travels with cold blood. And I hope nothing worse.'

With the Fathermacdonalt's help, he climbed up the little ladder to the door of the hut. The pig snuffed away underneath them, in the space between the stilts. He wasn't sure if the pig was real, or if he'd added it for his dream. The pig snuffed.

'I'm glad you came, Andrew. That is, I would always be glad, but now I am especially so.'

He had smiled and drunk the soup he'd been given. It seemed very hot to his tongue, but his hands round the bowl felt perfectly cool. They seemed to be a little numb.

'I thought I might have lost you there, Andrew, going off to the One Handed Man. I thought I might have lost you. And you always were my favourite. I shouldn't have favourites, but there you go, I do. That's why I called you Andrew. You know that?'

He knew that.

'Andrew, for the Patron Saint of Scotland. Because Scotland is my home, or was. I was your age when I left it and I'm not going to see it again. What do you think of that, eh? I'm going to die here, Andrew, before anyone remembers where I am and decides to call me back. I think I shall die quite soon and be buried very comfortably. Here.'

He looked at the Fathermacdonalt and wanted to touch him. He wanted to put his hand on the white, white hair the old man had grown all around his head. Perhaps it would comfort the Fathermacdonalt, if he was going to die. And it would let him feel what the hair was like. Perhaps to kiss the Fathermacdonalt would be best. He wasn't sure.

'Would you mind if I talked to you a little? I'm sure you have other things to do, but I would like it if you could stay. Could you, Andrew? And I think you should stay a while longer. You're very pale.'

'I can stay.'

'Thank you. It's not that I want to tell you about Scotland. It's too different and you'd find it too strange. But it's very like here. That's what I want you to know. Everywhere is very like here. Places are the same because you don't change. Do you understand?'

'No. At least I understand, but I think something else.'

'I know. I did, too. Because I was like you. I was so like you.

16

My mother used to sing to me. She used to teach me things in the old language of our country, the language, I suppose, of my tribe. I learned about black huts, burning and the Killing Times. I learned about the hills and valleys where we used to live and the animals that took our place. I learned about green things, but I lived in a black city, a city where the rain would hang in the streets, because the air was so thick with black. So I began to dream of green things and of coming here and, although I spoke the language of the black city, my mother's green words were safe inside me.

'I was allowed to go from my country to Spain. The country of the Conquistadors. For years and years, since other bad times in Scotland, there had been a kind of school there where young men like me could go and learn to be priests and prepare for our mission here, in the Americas. But first we had to learn to be Spanish, like the Conquistadors. Before I left there I thought and prayed and preached and dreamed in Spanish. Even when we played football, remember I showed you that, even the football was in Spanish. And, when I left, I felt I was leaving home. But those green words were still inside me, too.

'When I came here, over miles of ocean, nothing but water anywhere, I had to learn all over again. Your Spanish was different, your cities were strange. But the women carrying babies wrapped in their shawls, they were the same. The beggars, the drunken men, the sadness and the anger in the songs and running in the gutterless street, they were familiar. They had come with me, through Scotland and Spain.

'Then I came to you. After too many years I came to you, where everything is so green and I began to remember my mother's songs. I've wasted most of my life trying to get here and, now I have, I'm back where I began. Green words.

'I suppose I should be sad but I'm not. My countrymen have died in the Americas and in Spain. I can die here. Here is home, too. Andrew?'

'Yes?'

'I would like to sing to you.'

'I would like that.'

'Good.'

And that was the dream.

When it had finished, he lay, curled in to his stomach and the blanket across his face. The One Handed Man softly pulled the cover back to kiss his forehead and then his cheek.

'You are very cold, young man, young Andrew; very cold and very pale. They'll give you a new name when you go home. They'll call you the Dead Man. Will you like that?'

'I don't know. I don't think so.'

'It could be worse, though. And it'll keep you safe. The dead are always safe. They are left alone. You know who you are, really?'

'Yes.'

'Then what does it matter? You've only made a journey and come back a little changed. What did you dream?'

'The Fathermacdonalt.'

'Mm hm. And what do you do when you see the dead and then dream about someone?'

'You should...the dead want revenge. You should kill whoever you dream, then the dead will be satisfied. Is that right?'

'Maybe. Have you done that before?'

'No.'

'And do you want to kill Father MacDonald?'

'No.'

'Then don't.'

'I don't understand.'

'The dream only meant you should go and see him. Go and do that. Oh, and don't come back.'

'What? What did I do? What have I done? Why can't I come back?'

'Because you don't belong here. You mean you want to come back? Hmm? So fuck off. You know what that means? It's Yanqui for goodbye. Goodbye, Dead Man. Take your magic with you when you go.'

And a last kiss.

'Go on.'

When he had looked back to the hut, walking away, it was too dark inside to be sure there was anyone there. When he looked back again, there were trees, fallen and growing, nothing but trees and the green dark and dampness of trees. He went home.

It had been very quiet almost all the way there. Birds would clatter, close by when he passed them, when they were disturbed, but otherwise they were quiet. Even the leaves were quiet. Had he not felt hungry he would have believed he was dreaming again and dreaming badly, forgetting there should be sounds.

Because he couldn't smell a storm coming he knew there must be something wrong and thought he should go home to warn them. He decided to hurry and do that. But, of course, as he ran along paths that grew more and more familiar – the mud so very soft – he could smell that what was wrong was waiting ahead. It was at home.

All the huts had been burned. At first he was glad. Huts could always be built again, there was always wood. Then he turned to walk on through the ashes and saw the hand. It was a curled little monkey hand, lying palm up, black in the black ash of his second uncle's home. When he looked there were also feet. There were bones. There were pieces of things.

He was glad that whoever had done this had burned the bodies, along with the huts. This way there weren't dead faces to stare at him, familiar. But, when he had sat for a while and looked at his own curled hands, palms up, he wished they had left the bodies alone, because he wanted something to hold now, something to kiss.

'What are you doing there, are you sleeping?'
The Fathermacdonalt came closer. The light ran along the corn leaves, like water, just as it had before, and the Fathermacdonalt would take him inside now and want to give him soup.

The girl stirred, stretched. Perhaps he was disturbing her. His unpleasant words were making her wake, or dream, making her uneasy. He didn't want to tell her how he had broken his own dream.

He wouldn't do that.

He could do it. He could sit and imagine the machete with the half burned handle and the unrepeatable noise of it meeting

19

the Fathermacdonalt, surprising him and sending him to join the dead. He could let that out of his mouth in words. But he wouldn't. It was too late now. It was enough that he had killed an old man for bringing his country with him when he travelled. He had found the spent bullets amongst the other fragments in the ash and known that the Fathermacdonalt had infected them all with Scotland and now all the homes would burn and all the people would go and the farmers would turn the whole of it into grass and then barrenness.

When he wasn't angry any more he went back to the body and stroked its hair where there wasn't blood. It was too soft on the head. It hardly felt of anything at all, and on the face, it was too hard, like a pig's hair. He dug a grave for the Fathermacdonalt and hoped that it would please him and his spirit would be content. He didn't kiss him although he would have been able to.

'You are a lost soul.'
He knew that.
'Your soul is lost.'
Which was the same thing.
'Without the good news of Jesus, without that honey sweet, burning bright message of light and eternal life planted deep in your heart, deep down in your very heart, you will remain lost, cast out in the wilderness and condemned to the pains and fires and the torments of Hell.

'Do you think that God never saw you – you and your wickedness and nakedness and your stench of sin? Do you think he didn't long to punish you? Do you think he didn't look down and long to cry out, "Behold, they shall be as stubble: the fire shall burn them: they shall not deliver themselves from the power of the flame."?

'And didn't you burn? Didn't you burn? Your houses, your villages and your forests, didn't you burn? And still you do not repent.

'"Therefore evil shall come upon thee: thou shalt not know from whence it riseth: and mischief shall fall upon thee: thou shalt not be able to put it off: and desolation shall come upon thee suddenly which thou shalt not know."

'Allow me to tell you a little about Hell.'

It had taken a long time for him to come to the New Mission to Indians. When he ran through their fields in the dark they seemed to be no different from the other places where the trees were ripped back and the farmers had a hold on the land. Except there were no dogs. In all the other places they had dogs. They wouldn't bite him, they would only come near enough to smell how dead he was, but their howling and whimpering would bring the Ladino farmers out with guns. The New Mission to Indians had no dogs, only people.

Two of these had found him, asleep and still running in his sleep, about to have a fever and let starvation take its course. He was taken inside the palisade, clothed and fed and cared for. They only began to tell him about Hell when he was strong enough to stand.

He took up the life of a mission indian. As soon as the sun had risen a bell would wake them and a strange, disorderly tribe would go to have its breakfast in the scrubbed, wooden hall. Men sat on one side, women on the other, both sides restless and somehow lost in their new, modest clothes. When their bowls had been cleared they would sit very still, inside yawning collars and shirts whose sags and wrinkles dissolved shoulders and annihilated breasts and they would hear the Good News about Hell.

The tribe flapped and sagged through polishing, cooking, scrubbing, building, planting and the learning of strange songs. This was interrupted by two other meals, two more talks about Hell and the terrible ritual of washing and soap.

At the end of every day, the bell returned. The tribe would kneel in the hall, sing a song and go back to its dormitories, ready to start again. The men and women slept in separate buildings, but the same words were painted in gold letters on the walls of each.

THIS YE SHALL HAVE OF MY HAND: YE SHALL LIE DOWN IN SORROW.

Only a few of them could read it, but they all knew what it meant.

The Hell talks didn't bother him, nor the orderly existence and the unruly clothes, the slow coating of his senses with dusty

21

polish and soap. It was only when he lay on his hard, still dormitory bed that he would think of eternal life and know he was terrified.

But the New Mission to Indians fed him and let him feel his strength again. It came as no surprise when none of the others would work with him or when the men who had to sleep near him were troubled with dreams. His paleness and his thin, cold limbs even worried the Yanqui men, although not as much as Hell and nakedness seemed to do. He was called, as he had expected, the Dead Man, and was content to spend his time eating, listening, scrubbing and polishing. And sometimes he swept.

He only left after the women came back. They were there in the morning one day before sunrise. The dawn uncovered them, damp, lying in each other's arms by the palisade. The two of them.

Almost a year ago they had run away from the New Mission. That's what he heard. Now one of them sat in the scrubbed hall again, quiet, but still a little proud and wearing the clothes she had arrived in; a tight, slithering sheath of coloured cloth. The rest of the tribe flapped and stared at her.

The women had gone to the city. They had run away to whatever the city was, returning with dark eyes and strange clothes. One of them had also brought an open gash along her thigh. She now lay in the hospital, bandaged. On the journey back through the forest, the wound had begun to rot and perhaps she would lose her leg, perhaps she would die. In the talks about Hell that day and for many days after, they were assured that she would die. The Yanqui men would stare at the one remaining woman, now suitably buried in cloth.

'Thou hast polluted thy land with thy whoredoms and thy wickedness.'

On the sixth day the woman in hospital stopped screaming and on the seventh day, she died. He saw her, beautifully dead and new, ripening into flight and the glass beads on the heel of each shoe winked as she walked up and up.

He watched her leave and knew he should follow her.

After that evening's Hell talk, as the tribe fluttered off to bed, he called out, so that the Yanqui men would look at him, and he flew. He felt their watching and turned in the air above them with a smile. They must have been very surprised. He liked that. And he enjoyed their fear.

Tch. Tch. Tch.

In his mind and certainly in the minds of the Yanqui men, Hell and the distant city had become interchangeable. As he walked towards it, first through shrivelled trees and then across naked brown, the landscape seemed increasingly familiar. But the city, when he found it, wasn't Hell. They were wrong to call it that. It was home. His bloodless face was only one among thousands here and his thin limbs were no closer to the bone than many others. Here they were all dead and were all as safe as the dead for as long as they managed to live by their rules. Only no one ever could.

The girl snatched in her breath, preparing to wake, and then opened her eyes. She looked a little frightened. Perhaps she had heard too much of his voice. But she didn't seem hurt, it seemed she was well.

It was raining now. A pouring weight of grey water was scouring the streets deeper into the mud and beginning to undermine some of its walls. People would be drowned tonight and then, tomorrow, the mud would slide and bury some of the city and its people, dead and alive.

The rain could have woken her; it was very loud. Perhaps she was afraid of the rain. She shouldn't be.

Night geometry and the Garscadden trains

One question.

Why do so many trains stop at Garscadden? I don't mean stop. I mean finish. I mean terminate. Why do so many trains terminate at Garscadden?

Every morning I stand at my station, which isn't Garscadden, and I see them: one, two, three, even four in a row, all of them terminating at Garscadden. They stop and no one gets off, no one gets on; their carriages are empty, and then they pull away again. They leave. To go to Garscadden. To terminate there.

I have never understood this. In the years I have waited on the westbound side of my station, the number of trains to Garscadden has gradually increased; this increase being commensurate with my lack of understanding. The trees across the track put out leaves and drop leaves; the seasons and the trains to Garscadden pass and I do not understand.

It's stupid.

So many things are stupid, though. Like the fact that the death of my mother's dog seemed to upset me more than the death of my mother. And I loved my mother more than I loved her dog. The stupidity of someone being killed by the train that might normally take them home, things like that. There seems to be so much lack of foresight, so much carelessness in the world. And people can die of carelessness. They lack perspective.

24

I do, too. I know it. I am the most important thing in my life. I am central to whatever I do and those whom I love and care for are more vital to my existence than statesmen, or snooker players, or Oscar nominees, but the television news and the headlines were the same as they always are when my mother died and theirs were the names and faces that I saw. Nations didn't hold their breath and the only lines in the paper for her were the ones I had inserted.

Inserted. Horrible word. Like putting her in a paper grave.

To return to the Garscadden trains, they are not important in themselves; they are only important in the ways they have affected me. Lack of perspective again, you see? Naturally, they make me late for work, but there's altogether more to them than that. It was a Garscadden train that almost killed my husband.

Of course you don't know my husband, Duncan, and I always find him difficult to describe. I carry his picture with me sometimes; more to jog my memory than through any kind of sentiment. I do love him. I do love him, even now. I love him in such a way that it seems, before I met him, I was waiting to love him. But I remember what I remember and that isn't his face.

Esau was an hairy man. I remember my mother saying that. It always sounded more important than just saying he was born with lots of hair. I only mention Esau now, because Duncan wasn't hairy at all.

He had almost no eyebrows, downy underarm hair and a disturbingly naked chest. We used to go walking together as newly weds, mainly on moorland and low hills where he'd been as a scout. The summers were usually brief, unsettled, the way you'd expect, but the heat across the moors could be remarkable. It seems to be a quality of moors. The earth is warm and sweaty under the wiry grass, the heather bones are brilliant white and the sun swings, blinding, overhead. You walk in a cloud of wavering air and tiny, black insects.

On such days – hot days – Duncan would never wear a T-shirt. Not anything approaching it. He would put on a shirt, normally pale blue or white, roll the sleeves up high on his arms and wear the whole thing loose and open like a jacket, revealing a thin, vulnerable chest. Sensible boots, socks, faded khaki shorts and the shirt flapping: he would look like those embarrassing forties photographs of working class men at the beach or in desert armies. He had a poverty stricken chest, pale with little boy's skin.

There was hair on his head, undoubtedly, honey brown and cut short enough to subdue the natural curl, but his face was naked. I remember him washing and brushing his teeth, but I don't believe he ever shaved. There was no need.

Duncan, you might also notice, is in the past tense – not because he's dead, because he's over. I call him my husband because I've never had another one and everything I tell you will only show you how he was. Today I am a different person and he will be, too. Whatever I describe will be part of our past. I used to want to own his past. I used to want to look after him retrospectively. This was during the time when our affair had turned into marriage but still had something to do with love. In fact, there was a lot of love about. I mean that.

My clearest memory of him comes from about that time. I don't see it, because I never looked at it. I only remember a feeling, safe and complete, of lying with him, eyes closed, and whispering that I wanted to own his past; that I wanted to own him, too.

It was strange. However we flopped together, however haphazardly we decided to come to rest, the fit would always be the same.

His right arm, cradling my neck.

My head on his shoulder.

My right arm across his chest.

My left arm, tucked away between us with my hand resting quietly on his thigh. Not intending to cause disturbance, merely resting, proprietary.

In these pauses, we would doze together before sleeping and dreaming apart and we would whisper. We always whispered, very low and very soft, as if we were afraid of disturbing each other.

'I love you.'
'Uh hu.'

26

'I do love you.'
'I know that. I feel that. I love you, too.'
'I want to look after you.'
'You can't.'
'Why not.'
'Because I'm looking after you.'
'That's alright, then.'
'I love you.'
'Uh hu.'
'I do love you.'

And, finally, we would be quiet and sleepy and begin to breathe in unison. I've noticed since, if you're very close to anything for long enough, you'll start to breathe in unison. Even my mother's dog, when he slept with his head on my lap, would eventually breathe in time with me. There was more to it than that with Duncan, of course.

I sometimes imagined our hearts beat together, too. It's silly, I know, but we felt close then. Closer than touch.

This positioning, our little bit of night geometry, this came to be important in a way I didn't like because it changed. I didn't like it then, as much as I now don't like to remember the two of us together and almost asleep, because, by fair means or foul, you can't replace that. Intensity is easy, it's the simple nearness that you'll miss.

The change happened one evening on a Sunday. We had cocoa in bed. I made it in our little milk pan and I whisked it with our little whisk, to make it creamy, and we drank it sitting up against the pillows and ate all butter biscuits, making sure we didn't drop any crumbs. There is nothing worse than a bed full of crumbs. And we put away the cocoa mugs and we turned out the lights and that was fine. Very nice.

But when we slowed to a stop, when we terminated, the geometry had changed. I didn't really think about it because it was so nicely changed.

My right arm around his neck.

His head against my shoulder.

His one arm tucked between us very neat, and the other, just resting, doing nothing much, just being there.

It all felt very pleasant. The good weight of him, snuggled

27

down there, the smell of his hair when I kissed the top of his head. I did that. I told him I could never do enough, or be enough, or give enough back and I kissed the top of his head. I told him I belonged to him. I think he was asleep.

I told him anyway and he was my wee man, then, and I couldn't sleep for wanting to look after him.

The following morning, I waited on the westbound platform and the smell of him was still on me, even having washed. All that day when I moved in my clothes, combed my hair, his smell would come round me as if he'd just walked through the room.

It was good, that. Not unheard of in itself, hardly uncommon, in fact. It wasn't unknown for me to leave my bed and dress without washing in order to keep what I could of the night before, but you'll understand that, this time, I was remembering something special. I thought, unique.

Now I realise that you can never be sure that anything is unique. You can never be sure you know enough to judge. I mean, when Pizzaro conquered the Incas, they thought he was a god – his men, too – when really Spain was full of Spaniards just like him. Eventually you see you were mistaken, but look what you've had to lose in order to learn.

I thought that the way I met Duncan was unique.

Wrong.

Not in the place: a bar. Not in the time: round about eight. Not in the circumstances: two friends of friends, talking at a wee, metal table when the rest of the conversation dipped. It was a bit of a boring evening to tell the truth.

We all left on the bell for last orders and there was the usual confusion about coats – who was sitting on whose jacket, who'd lost gloves. Duncan and I were a little delayed, quite possibly not by chance.

'I'm going to call you tomorrow. Ten o'clock. 'What's your number?'

'What?'

'What number could I get you on, tomorrow at ten o'clock?'

'In the morning?'

'Yes, in the morning.'

'Well, I would be at work, then.'

'I know that, what's the number?'

28

I gave him the office number and he went away. I don't even think he said goodbye.

At a quarter to eleven, the following day, he called McSwiggin and Jones and was put through to me. I had some idea that he might be in need of advice. McSwiggin and Jones accepted payment from various concerns with money to call in the debts of various individuals without it. Debt, as Mr McSwiggin often said, could be very democratic – Mrs Gallacher with two small boys, no husband and her loan from the Social Fund turned down was in debt. And so was Peru. Perhaps, I thought, Duncan was in debt.

'What do you mean, in debt?'

'I mean, who do you owe money? I can't help you if it's on our books. I mean I can, but not really, you know.'

'No, I don't know. I owe my brother a fiver, since you ask.'

'Mm hm.'

'And that's it. I don't have any debts, just a bit of an overdraft which doesn't count. I want to see you tonight. I could bring my bank statement with me if you'd like.

'Look, I'm sorry, but you're wasting my time, aren't you?'

'I'm sorry if you feel that way. I thought we got on well together.'

'Ring me at home tomorrow evening. This is ridiculous and I'm at work.'

He called at the end of the week and we went out for a coffee on the Sunday afternoon. Before I had time to ask he told me that he and Claire, his partner from the pub, were only friends. They'd been at school together which is why they'd seemed so close the other evening.

When Duncan and I were married, quite a while later, Claire was at the little party afterwards. She smiled quietly when she saw me, danced with Duncan once and then left. I had to ask who she was because she looked so familiar, but I couldn't remember her name.

So, Duncan and I were married and we were unique. Although men and women often marry as an expression of various feelings and beliefs and although they often go to bed

29

together before, during and after marriage, the thing with Duncan and me was unrepeatable, remarkable and entirely unique. So I thought.

No one had ever married us before and we had never married each other. It was tactfully assumed that the going to bed had happened with other partners in other times, but they had never managed to reach the same conclusion. We were one flesh, one collection of jokes and habits and one smell. Even now, I know, the smell of my sweat and the taste of my mouth are not the same as they were before I met him. He will always be that much a part of me, whether I like it or not.

Even when two different friends in two different ladies toilets in two different bars told me that Claire and Duncan had been sleeping and staying awake together for months before I met him, I didn't mind. I didn't mind if they had continued to see each other after we met. I was flattered he had taken the trouble to lie. It didn't matter because he had left her for me and we had made each other unique.

Finally, of course, I realised the most original things about us were our fingerprints. Nothing of what we did was ever new. I repeated the roles that Duncan chose to give me in his head – wicked wife, wounded wife, the one he would always come back to, the one he had to leave and I never even noticed. I always felt like me. For years, I never knew that when he rested with his head on my shoulder, all wee and snuggled up, it was helping him to ease his guilt. Once or twice a year, it was his body's way of saying he'd been naughty, but he was going to be a good boy from now on.

And I was a good wife. I even answered the telephone with a suitably unexpected voice, to give his latest girlfriend her little shiver before she hung up. Like a good wife should.

All the time I thought I was just being married when, really, Duncan was turning me into Claire and the ones before and after Claire.

I lived with the only person I've met who can snore when he's wide awake, who soaked his feet until they looked like a dead man's, then rubbed them to make them peel. I've washed hundreds of towels, scaley with peelings from his feet. I've cooked him nice puddings, nursed him through the 'flu, stopped him trimming his fringe with the kitchen scissors and

30

have generally been a good wife. Never knowing how Duncan saw me inside his head. It seems I was either a victim, an obstacle or a safety net. I wasn't me. He took away me.

But it wasn't his fault, not really. It was the E numbers in his yoghurt, or his role models when he was young. It was a compulsion. Duncan, the wee pet lamb, would chase after anything silly enough to show him a half inch of leg. From joggers to lady bicyclists to the sad looking Scottish Nationalist who sold papers round the pubs in his kilt. Duncan couldn't help it. It wasn't his fault .

I sound like an idiot, not seeing how things were for so long. I felt like an idiot, too. Nothing makes you feel more stupid than finding out you were wrong when you thought you were loved. The first morning after I discovered, it wasn't good to wake up. Over by the wall in the bedroom there was a wardrobe with a mirror in the door. I swung my legs out of bed and just sat. There I was; reflected; unrecognisable. I looked for a long while until I could tell it was me: pale and slack, round shouldered and dank-haired, varicose veins, gently mapping their way. You would have to really love me to like that and Duncan, of course, no longer loved me at all. I could have felt sorry for him, if I hadn't felt so sorry for myself.

I considered the night before and letting his head rest on my shoulder, knowing what I finally knew. It was as if I wasn't touching him, only pressing against his skin through a coating of other women. I'd felt his breath on my collar bone and found it difficult not to retch.

It had taken about a month to fit all the pieces together in my head. Nothing silly like lipstick on collars, or peroxide blonde hairs along his lapels: it was all quite subtle stuff. He would suddenly become more crumpled, as if he had started sleeping in his shirts, while his trousers developed concertina creases and needed washing much more regularly. The angle of the passenger seat in the car would often change and, opening the door in the morning, there would be that musty smell. And yet, for all the must and wrinkles, the fluff all over his jackets, as if they'd been thrown on the floor, Duncan would be taking pains with his appearance. When he walked out of the flat he'd never looked better and when he returned he'd never looked worse. Life seemed to be treating him very roughly, which perhaps explained his sudden interest in personal hygiene, the increasingly frequent washing and the purchase of bright, new Saint Michael's underwear. It's all very obvious now, but it wasn't then. Even though it had been repeating itself for years.

Duncan's infidelity didn't have all the implications it might have today. I didn't take a blood test, although I've watched for signs of anything since. Still, you can imagine the situation in the first few weeks with both of us constantly washing away the feel of his current mistress. We went through a lot of soap.

I suppose that I should have left him, or at least made it clear that I'd found him out. I should have made sure that we both knew that I knew what he knew. Or whatever it was you were meant to make sure of. I didn't know. To tell the truth, it didn't really seem important. It was to do with him and things to do with him didn't seem important any more. I couldn't see why he should know what was going on inside my head when, through all the episodes of crumpled shirts and then uncrumpled shirts and even the time when he tried for a moustache, I had never had any idea of what Duncan was thinking.

I stayed and, for a long time, things were very calm. We finished with all of our washing, started to sleep at night and I managed to get the dryer to chew up six pairs of rainbow coloured knickers. Duncan went back to being just a little scruffy and always coming home for tea.

It wasn't going to last, I knew. It would maybe be a matter of months before the whole performance started up again and I wasn't sure how I would react to that. In the meantime I sorted out my past. I still worked at McSwiggin and Jones, but only for three days out of seven and instead of spending the rest of my week on housework or other, silly, things I started to sit on the bed a lot and stare at that mirror door. I bought some books on meditation and, at night, when I felt Duncan sleeping, I used to breathe the way they told me to – independently. It wasn't easy, crumpling up a marriage and throwing it away, looking for achievements I'd made that weren't to do with being a wife, but I don't think I did too badly. For a while I was a bit depressed, but only a bit.

My future, and this surprised me, was much harder to redefine. All the hopes you collect: another good holiday abroad, a proper fitted kitchen, children, a child. Your future creates an atmosphere around you and mine was surprisingly beautiful. Duncan and I, retired, would grow closer and closer, more and more serene, there would be grandchildren, picnics, gardening and fine, white hair. There would be trust and understanding, dignity in sickness and not dying alone. We would leave good things behind us when we were gone. I can't imagine where it all came from, I only know that it was hard to give away.

Then, one Monday morning, there was an incident involving my husband and a Garscadden train.

I went down, as usual, to stand on the westbound platform, this time in a hard, grey wind, the black twigs and branches over the line, oily and dismal with the damp. I waited in the little, orange shelter, read the walls and watched the Garscadden trains. There were three, and a Not In Service and, for the first time in my life, I gave up the wait. I turned around, walked away from the shelter and went home. I wished it would rain. I wanted to feel rain on my face.

The hall still smelt of the toast for breakfast. I took off my coat and went into the bedroom, needing to look in the mirror again, and there they were, in bed with the fire on, nice and cosy: Duncan and a very young lady I had never met before. They seemed to be taking the morning off. Duncan ducked his head beneath the bedclothes, as if I wouldn't know it was him, and she stared at the shape he made in the covers and then she stared at me.

I don't believe I said a single word. There wasn't a word I could say. I don't remember going to the kitchen, but I do remember being there, because I reached into one of the drawers beside the sink and I took out a knife. To be precise, my mother's old carving knife. I was going to run back to the bedroom and do what you would do with a carving knife, maybe to one of them, maybe to both, or perhaps just cut off his prick. That thought occurred.

That thought and several others and you shouldn't pause for thought on these occasions. I did and that was it. In the end I tried to stab the knife into the worksurface, so that he would see it there, sticking up, and know that he'd had a near miss. The point slid across the formica and my hand went down on the blade, so that all of the fingers began to bleed. When

Duncan came in, there was blood everywhere and my hand was under the tap and I'm sure he believed I'd tried to kill myself. The idea seemed to disturb him, so I left it at that.

He drove me to and from the hospital and stayed that night in the flat, but, when he was sure I felt stable again, he went away and we began the slow division of our memories and ornaments. It was all done amicably, with restraint, but we haven't kept in touch.

And that, I suppose, is the story of how my husband was almost killed by one Garscadden train too many. It is also the story of how I learned that half of some things is less than nothing at all and that, contrary to popular belief, people, many people, almost all the people, live their lives in the best way they can with generally good intentions and still leave absolutely nothing behind.

There is only one thing I want more than proof that I existed and that's some proof, while I'm here, that I exist. Not being an Olympic skier, or a chat show host, I won't get my wish. There are too many people alive today for us to notice every single one.

But the silent majority and I do have one memorial, at least. The Disaster. We have small lives, easily lost in foreign droughts, or famines; the occasional incendiary incident, or a wall of pale faces, crushed against grillwork, one Saturday afternoon in Spring. This is not enough.

The moving house

Grace drinks and feels the water from the tap and finds it sweet.
That means her mouth is sour. She feels sick.

She can remember dreaming, although she doesn't think she
slept. She wouldn't have slept. But the dream is sharp in her
mind, as if it had happened again in sleep and she had seen what
she always did see – a door, opened smoothly on a room with
the curtains drawn. The familiar dream.

Think of something else to keep it away. The first thing you
remember: think of that. Cold of the cold tap laid along your
cheek and think of that.

Your father.

Grace's father went away when she was small and didn't
write letters, or a postcard, or come back. There is only one
memory she has of him; the first she has of anything, full stop.
The first thing she knows that happened to her.

The sitting room was dark and the curtains were drawn –
night time dogs and cars outside them. Everything she looked
at was changed and dim and being there was like a secret: a
private thing, between the two of them.

Her father had carried her, up out of bed in his arms, her feet
in his jacket pockets, his shoulder under her head. She remembers
the bitter smell of his shirt, warm breath and his hands beneath

35

and behind her, holding her up. He sat with her on his lap, in the deep armchair and the skin of his face was rough but not rough. She pressed against it a little, to be sure. Her hand in his was good, surrounded, and Grace fell asleep by the rise and fall of his chest. When she woke, it was finished. She didn't have any more of him after that.

A few years on from when he left them and Grace was gone, too. Maybe at the time they didn't tell her, but it seemed they hadn't meant it like that. She just went away to Aunt Ivy's, took a wee case, and slowly, other things of hers would follow. The day they bought a bed for her she knew that she would stay.

She slept in the front room, first on the folding-down sofa and then on her own, bought bed. Her aunt would have moved away the china – her good things and her glass – but she never did, because Grace was a careful child. I'll put them away, Grace. You'll break them.

I promised, I won't. They're better out. You like them like that. If you break one, just one thing, then all of them go.

Clear eyes, looking up.

Uh hu.

So Grace's room had vases and white linen and dark wood. Together, they emptied drawers for her own stuff and, in the day, she had a coverlet and cushions to put on the bed. It was prettier than the couch; they both thought that. In the late afternoons, Grace would stand in her wide, bay window and watch the light in the ruby crystal bowl, its rim hung with clear, glass drops. She liked to see the colours on the tablecloth: the curves of red and white, and it wasn't hers, it was hers to look after which was different and made it special; something to do with love.

More. You want more of that. Brush your hair and brush your teeth. Quiet, and the pain won't come. You should sit.

Grace saying Auntie Ivy wasn't right: Ivy was her mother's mother's sister, which made her a Great Aunt. And Ivy would have been a great aunt, anyway; That was their joke. If Grace ever wanted something, she only had to say

Please, Great Aunt

and the skin across Ivy's nose would redden and, most times, the answer would be yes. It was too easy, so Grace didn't say it a lot.

Difficult parts; there were difficult parts as well. Her aunt worked in the hospital, cleaning and the hours for that were queer. Halfway through the afternoon, she started and then she wasn't home until the night. This was good in the mornings, because nobody was hurrying but Grace and going to school could be slow and quite nice. The problem was coming home to an empty house.

Letting herself in was lonely.

No, don't remember that. Not waking too late in the morning with no breakfast smell and no radio and everything too late. Something had been altered while she slept and now it was wrong. So she went to her auntie's room and let herself in and it smelt of talcum and camphor and hand cream which wasn't a change, but she felt there was something missing, or something replaced. There was a new smell there now, a smell you could almost see. She'd been expecting it, because you shouldn't trust old people, they always die, and as soon as she opened the door, she knew.

Back at the start, the beginning. Remember that.

At the start Mrs Cruickshank from down the stair had wanted to take her in; just for those hours in the evening when Grace was alone. Mrs Cruickshank's own children could be seen in ranks on her mantelpiece; smiling progressively older smiles, and she had a piano that played itself from a cardboard roll. That was nice. But Grace said, very nicely, that she wanted to learn how to cook and she asked for a key of her own to Aunt Ivy's flat.

Letting herself in was lonely, in the winter it was dark, and it seemed as if no one else lived there – as if she could wait and no one else would come. She would turn on the television set in the kitchen and go and do her homework in her room, with the sound of other voices at her back. Then she would change and go to stay in the kitchen with the talking and the fire, make a cup of tea and have a snack, nothing too much. The meal would always wait until her aunt was back and, unless the bus was late, Grace would have it ready, just right.

Both of them would have stories from where they had been.

They would eat and speak and listen a while and eat.

'This is very good, Grace.'

'Of course.'

'You weren't so hot on Monday.'

'Monday was a new thing, maybe it should be like that.'

'Well, the recipe should have said so; I'd have put in an old pair of teeth.'

He was smiling, you saw him, how he smiled. The eyes were closed and the lips were back from the teeth. A smile looks like that.

Why did you come here, back to your mother? They said you were going home, but it never was home and you grew up into you somewhere else. If you'd been older, if you could have left the school. With a job, they would have let you stay away, but nobody gets jobs now, not straight out of school, not proper jobs. You'll be out on the street, or stuck here for life. Whichever way, you'll be nothing. You won't be anything.

It was lonely, letting herself in, but that black, lonely feeling: it turned itself inside out. Not sure when. It began to be waiting whenever you left the flat. People out there, you could tell, there was something about them, making them hard. You were only safe with old folk, the ones with other lessons learned. That, or sitting in the blocks of sun, through the kitchen window and being just quiet and by yourself.

Not that she'd really wanted to be by herself, but Ivy had started shrinking away, long before she was ill. There came a lightness in her movements that frightened Grace. She came into a room and her body apologised: her eyes would say she was sorry for being old. Aunt Ivy now finished everyday tasks as if she was saying goodbye and it hurt to share a room with her, watching her tire.

Grace sits on the toilet and the pain seems suddenly fresh. She sees the blood, is sick, cold after.

Don't stay here. Get out. You mustn't be late. They'll ask why, if you're late.

She goes to put on her uniform. It has stayed the same, a children's thing, it should be that it no longer fits.

She presses her hands against her head.

Something good. Something good.

The day they saw the rainbow, that was good. Because of the times Auntie Ivy worked, Sunday was their day. They made it important and kept it to themselves: a proper Sunday Lunch and then the park to walk it off. When they went out that day, the sun shone, it was hot, but there was thunder in it, you could tell. Then it rained and they were caught out – the rain so fast and so wet that it was funny. Fresh.

'Will you look at that. A rainbow. A whole one, Gracie, there.'

They took the path on the rise, until they could see it all: hazy arching over, then thick and shining colour near the ground. Grace said they were daft, but she was smiling, and Ivy told her not to be so old. They couldn't get any wetter – not now.

At home, Grace lit the summer fire she had laid in the kitchen and they sat in their dressing gowns with tea.

She doesn't want to pass the room. The door will be closed: he closed it, but she doesn't want to pass the room. If she carries her shoes, doesn't wear them, he won't hear. She paces up and down the stairs in stocking feet, don't slip, don't stop. At the bottom, her head is spinning and she bends forward, holding her ache. From the room above her, no sound.

Grace had been in charge of the fires. She knew how to make them fetched coal up in the bucket and chopped wood. Her aunt had a joiner friend who came round, once a fortnight, with offcuts in a sack. Sometimes there was hardboard – hard to break up.

The joiner, Mr Taylor, had been a friend of Ivy's since the war. She always said he should stay for his tea and he always said that next time he would. He came to Aunt Ivy's funeral, right inside the crematorium, and Grace's mother laughed.

'Christ, is that old bugger still alive?'

Grace had wanted to speak to him afterwards, but Charlie and her mother took her away. She had wanted to turn round smile at him, but she couldn't get her mouth to work and, anyway, she couldn't smile – not there.

Charlie was her mother's friend, but her mother called him

Chick. He was the one who came with a van to take Grace's things from the flat. He was the one who moved her in.

The first night, all three of them had sat and watched TV. Chick went out and bought them fish suppers. His treat. Grace had tomato ketchup; burnt her tongue.

'I'll have to go to bed now. School.'

'Well, you now where it is – you're home now.'

Chick shouted up from the living room door.

'Night, night.'

Then she realised: he lived here, too. Later, their voices woke her through the wall. They made her feel far away from herself and sad.

This isn't the first time she's thought it, making the walk for the bus. She doesn't have to catch the one to school. There are buses to take her anywhere. Away: Dumbarton, Balloch, Oban, just away. Even on the right bus, she could stay in her seat and roll on past the stop.

But today, she wants to be there, where she knows things and it's warm. It's the bus that takes her home she wouldn't catch.

'Hiya, Gracie.'

'Hello.'

'Been out tonight, Gracie? Had a nice time? Is your mother back?'

'No, she's not.'

'So mummy's out on the town as well, uh hu?'

'I'm sorry, it's late, I was just going up.'

'Oh, don't do that, Gracie. I came home to see you.'

He dropped his head to one side and looked at her; frowned. As she went upstairs he took her arm.

Grace was glad it happened in their room not her own. Not her bed.

She looks at the bus ahead of hers and, across the back window, four boys. Their heads and backs are swaying all together. As if they were hearing a music that she can't. One of them turns and sees her, jerks up the finger, gives it a twist.

'Please, Grace, don't. You're a good girl. Don't tell her. If you tell her, she'll be angry. She'll be sad. Nobody has to know, Grace, please.'

She could hear that he was crying. As if he had taken everything

40

now; even the sounds she would make.

'Please, Grace. Grace. Fuckun say it. You won tell. You don even think about it.

'Stupid cunt. Nobody's gonny believe you. Who are you? You're fuckun nothun. See if they do believe you; they'll say it was your fault. You. Pretty, Gracie, fuckun you. Just you fuckun sleep on that. You do not tell. Think I couldn make it worse? You do not fuckun tell.'

He almost carried her out on to the landing; she didn't know if she could walk. The smell of him close again made her retch.

And in the morning, she could smell him on her and on her bed and in her sheets with the repeated rosebuds and the matching pillow case. The sheets that Auntie Ivy bought her in the summer. He had spoiled them, the way that he had spoiled her skin. She couldn't wash enough; he was in the bone and he came back like another dream.

'You'll get to like it, Gracie, all of us do.'

She had felt his hands across cheeks and his fingers in her hair.

'It's something you do with a friend, Grace, and I'm your friend. I'll be good to you. Don't worry, honey, the next time, it won't hurt.'

Genteel potatoes

This is no more than a story about Grandmother, because it cannot be the truth. If you and I were there to see it now, it might be the truth, but as it is, this is a story. Time divides me from my mother and her mother and beyond them there are lines and lines of women who are nothing more than shadows in my bones. And as you read this I am somewhere else. So this is a story.

In this story Grandmother will be afflicted by both her future and her past and the detail of her surroundings will be sadly incomplete. She will be there, perhaps with arthritic hands and a young girl's face, in a dress of no particular colour or shape, the streets around her very quiet, unsure of their proper sound.

Grandmother's age in the story is unclear. She is no younger than ten and no older than thirteen and is one of her parent's very many children. So far only one of them has died. Grandmother has no idea of which ones will leave the country and be buried in Canada, which ones will marry, which one will kill himself. She doesn't know them all that well.

Foremost among her numerous brothers and sisters are Edgar, Ivy and Sue.

Edgar, though only a boy, is bald-headed, stout and troubled very much with sciatica. He wears khaki overalls that smell of the turkeys he will keep.

Ivy is plump, cheerful, good at the waltz. She will have both of her hip joints replaced after an eighteen month wait, will make wonderful apple dumplings and be poor. She will be poorer than all of them, and almost all of them will be poor.

Sue, during the war, the Second War, that is, will find a severed head in the alley behind the house. The morning after the sugar works is bombed. What she will do with the head we do not know, but my mother will one day remember it when she sees another, severed head in a car crash in Dundee. No one she recognised.

Grandmother's mother who is one, whalebone stiff photograph today, will make my mother drink castor oil each time she goes to the dentist and once chased Grandmother all round the house with a riding crop for acknowledging the sex of the household cat, or for saying a pregnant lady was going to have a child. Possibly both. In these days suitable topics for conversation among young girls were rather restricted and the restrictions were rather vigorously applied.

And on this particular day of all those days, Grandmother – skinny, long-fingered, big-footed and possibly thirteen – would wake in the morning to the world of work. Her mother had told her that she would.

It had been decided that Grandmother's schooling had come to an end and now she would go into service and bring back a wage. She would cook and clean for a genteel lady and her genteel family and, as their genteel house was not so very far away, Grandmother could even go home and sleep in her own bed at night. This was a Good Position and Grandmother should be glad.

Grandmother was not glad. Grandmother had already whitewashed the kitchen ceiling while two pulleys of clean washing swung, inches away from her brush, just to prove it could be done. And she left the washing spotless, too. Nevertheless, she was once again pursued with the riding crop. And caught. But still she remained a wilful soul, naturally awkward with never the faintest idea of her station in life.

Only severe persuasion moved Grandmother from the front doorstep, along the street, around the corner and on the way to her first day's work. A great many tears were shed in the process and when, despite her best efforts, she did not get hopelessly lost, but arrived at her new employer's, safe and sound, she must have been a pitiable sight. All skin and bone and wet, pink, rabbit eyes.

The genteel lady of the house took her in and explained her duties very carefully. The genteel family had graduated from paying someone else to do their washing to employing a genuine, full time, domestic assistant. They were therefore, most particular whenever they laid down the law so that all those concerned could be sure they were born to it.

The genteel lady smiled a little, genteel smile for Grandmother, who stood very still; frail and amenable.

The work was not difficult, or easy, only familiar. Grandmother didn't dislike it – she had done it all before at home – but somehow her position filled her with a wearying kind of shame. There was no shame in cleaning, or cooking; no shame in service if you took to it. What seemed to trouble Grandmother was that she had one idea of service and the genteel lady seemed to have another. Grandmother was ashamed for being too hesitant to point out that difference.

The shame and the difference prayed on her mind but still, she scrubbed and polished and dusted and made everything shine with a suitably genteel shine. Then it was dinner time.

In the genteel kitchen were the huge, copper pans and the glossy, black range, all glowing with admiration for Grandmother's efforts in the hours before. Here, it was explained, Grandmother would cook dinner for the family and for herself. There were the genteel potatoes and there were the ones she could have. The lady of gentility would return in a while to see how the work progressed.

Of course the lady of the house was not fully in possession of the facts. No one ever is, but in this particular case, her ignorance would soon be her undoing.

And what does she not know?

Why, what we know.

That Grandmother now is fast approaching her eightieth year and yet she has never once, in all of that time, cooked an edible meal. That Grandmother is undeniably, a wilful soul, naturally awkward with never the faintest idea of her station in life.

That means that, if the dinner is cooked, the family may not

44

be poisoned, but they will be severely distressed. This also means that the dinner will never be cooked, because Grandmother is about to inspect the potatoes and find them wanting.

The genteel potatoes in the larger pile are soft and a little green and marked by careless lifting. Grandmother's very own potatoes are also soft and green and marked and, besides this, sprouting. Two of them have started to rot. Grandmother knows about potatoes. Her family keeps a little small holding and grows them. She is appalled by all these potatoes and appalled, more than anything else, by the potatoes which were set aside for her.

In her left hand, she snatches up a few of the family's potatoes. In her right, she flourishes two set aside for her; the soft rot from one of them, oozing through her fingers. Duly armed, she goes in search of her employer.

Bursting into the parlour, potatoes aloft, Grandmother fixes the genteel lady with one, magnificent glare. The same glare will, one day, wither tedious Methodist preachers at two hundred yards.

'See these?'

She will say, letting the middle class potatoes fall from her hand.

'We wouldn't feed these to our pigs.'

The family did keep pigs.

'And these...'

The proletarian potatoes make an overly soft landing on the rug and Grandmother is leaving her silence behind her. She has decided that she will resign. Nothing the genteel lady will ever say, and she will say a good deal, can change the fact that Grandmother resigned. She leaves voluntarily, shoulders back and remembering to take her coat. As she walks home there is no more shame and no more difference and the matter had been laid to rest.

Grandmother's mother will see her arriving home, hours too early, and go to fetch the riding crop. Grandmother's explanation will only make things worse and she will go to bed hungry, turn her back on her sister in bed and cry.

This won't be all her punishment. Next week she will be apprenticed to an old french polisher. He will be cruel to her, because he is a cruel man and because he is a drunkard. Worse

45

than this, Grandmother knows that she will be a drunkard, too. She will have to take the methylated spirits in her mouth and spit them out between her teeth to leave an even spray across the wood and, in the end, she'll get a taste for the meths, because all of them do. For months she will be very tired and very afraid.

But Grandmother will be saved. Someone will invent a mechanical, pressurised spray and she will begin to love her strange, man's job. She will learn to recognise every variety of wood, no matter how cleverly disguised. She will pluck out different shades of brown, like an eskimo identifying snow. She will make her living from almost invisible differences and will make each finished surface smoother than a dream of a whisper of a breath on silk. And still complain it's rough and shoddy work.

The first time she marries, no one will tell her that her husband has cancer and will die. He will be dead beside her the morning after their wedding night. It will be like a bad joke come true and nothing will be reliable again. For a long time she can't let herself be alone in her own home. She will willingly sit in the street in the rain, just to keep near to people as they pass.

Then Grandfather will marry her and love her very much and things will begin to get better, although never entirely the same. They will have their hair and their suits cut identically. Grandmother sports an Eton Crop for years. Their first and only child will be a daughter and her first and only child will be me.

That is how much will happen before Grandmother and I will even meet and before I can begin this story.

Didacus

These are a small people. On the whole, on the average, on the pavements, the people here are small.

Small in the body.

And we are speaking of a time here when small things were thought unimportant and the figures who now fill our bus stops were withered by lack of belief. In the larger world they were steadily forgotten and they woke up every morning, lost in their beds.

This is an early evening, caught in the teeth of a frost. October or later. In a graveyard to the West of the city a woman turns from the street and walks away. The cemetery has no lights and she is alone, but she thinks she wouldn't care, whatever happens. Just now she is looking for silence and somewhere dark to speak.

Please, God, be with us.

Help us to be good to each other.

The sky is clean and open and she feels she has a chance of getting through. On cloudy nights she doesn't bother and there's no point praying in the flat. There are seven other families above them and she doesn't have the energy to talk her way through that; she is, after all, a small woman.

They dug the older graves into the hillside, marking them with marble and sandstone. The woman is lost between the monuments and the incline hurts her legs. When the path evens out a little she can see the car, parked beneath the yew tree. Inside, a cigarette blinks alight.

'I've brought the mud in with me.'

'That's alright.'

He waits while she closes the door and settles herself in the seat.

'Kiss me, Jean.'

'No. No kissing.'

He sighs and throws his cigarette out of the window.

'Fine, then; just give me your hand.'

Jean helps unfasten the trousers and he rolls the seat back. Ready.

'At least you could tell me you want to.'

'Would I be here if I didn't.'

'Oh, Jean.'

She stares from behind his shoulder. A twist in the path leaves one stone out apart and she tries to fix her eyes on that. It belongs to a man called Didacus McGlone. She looked to find the name once, in daylight, and now she can remember it in the dark.

He takes her hand again.

'Did you?'

'Yes.'

'I didn't hear you.'

'Sometimes I don't make a noise.'

'If you want us to stop, you only have to tell me. You wouldn't lose your job. It isn't like that. I could move you up on the pay scale; get you an assistant for the lifting.'

'No.'

'OK Jean, OK. There's Kleenex in the glove compartment.'

'Thank you.'

'Will you let me drive you back?'

'No. What if Brian saw you?'

'What if?'

'You can't drive me back.'

'Do I really make you unhappy. You know you're free to do whatever you want…'

She opens the door and steps out. Sleet is falling.

'Jean? Have a safe journey home. We'll see you Monday morning.'

48

The small woman walks below the weather and feels the chill of the slurry underfoot. She wants to be back with her husband and this will make her late.

Please, God, let us be good for each other.

Brian is lying on the sofa and making machine tools in his head. He watches them turning and threading and smoothing. The swarf curls up towards him; perfect, like wax. It carries the eye clear away.

At one time he saved up his future and put it all in the cupboard at the end of the hall. He changed it into drill bits, micrometers, wonderful pieces of metal, heavy and precise. Their weight was a power in his hand.

His cupboard had been a place to be impatient; he would look at the piles of containers and lick his lips. Now when he passed he smelt oil and disappointment. Jean's cleaning stuff was in there, and other types of nonsense. He didn't mind.

Jean has a photograph of Brian. She keeps it in her handbag, but she knows it off by heart. It was taken in the first year they met.

He stands in his overalls, both hands in the pockets, smile at an angle and his weight on one leg. Behind him is the wooden fence from the bottom of her mother's garden and she knows from his face that the sun is bright and shining in his eyes.

Nothing has survived but the image.

The clock in the police station window is jerking towards half past ten. She wishes there were still buses running. The walk leaves her too much time to think.

The process of confinement and decay has been so gentle that their present situation still comes as a surprise. They are not without hope. Brian folds the sofa open, fetches out the sheets and knows that he can lie in, in the morning. Both of them are free each Sunday; at liberty to sleep and talk together.

That can't be bad.

He separates the pages of this evening's paper, then rolls them up and twists them for the fire. This way they burn slowly. He feeds on the first one to keep the glow alive. The rest can wait for Jean. He doesn't want to go to sleep without her, not tonight, but his hands are like dead things already and his eyes are letting go of the room.

Over Jean, the sky has turned the colour of yellow milk, so the praying will be over for tonight. The city is going to work, filling up the loans with footsteps and breathing. Maybe the year before there would have been conversation; room for a voice in the mouth. It's too late now for that.

Jean turns down the home street and tucks herself close to the wall. When she closes the door she wakes him.

'I'm sorry.'

'Jean?'

'Who else would it be?'

'You don't know who I'm expecting.'

'Yes I do. Did you have what I left you to eat?'

'No. I was too tired. Will it keep?'

He moves to start the fire again and she takes off her coat.

'There's no room in here with the bed down. It's like a padded cell.'

Brian throws the box of matches into the burning paper and the flare throws his shadow to the ceiling.

He sits on the mattress in the way that he sits when she knows that she has to go and hold him.

'Oh God.'

She would finish, but she knows there's no one near enough to hear.

'I kept them nice. I used to have nice hands. They were softer than yours. Always. Once we had the business started, no one would have known I'd ever worked.

His face is different from the photograph, but the eyes are almost the same. She pulls him to the side and takes his head on her lap. He keeps his fists curled to his stomach and the firelight swells the shadow, then the bone and then the shadow.

'Do they hurt you?'

'There's all metal in them again. I can't get it out.'

'I can, with a needle. I'll get all the pieces out. It's just you've got big fingers; you should leave it to me.'

'You never deserved this.'

The streets around them flatten under the wind as it rises and the final doors are locked until the morning. Low voices murmur; calling after dreams, while in other places, small

50

people run amongst machinery, their faces shut.

Jean and Brian hold each other and whisper, awake to taste the opening of the day.

They consider the freedom ahead.

Sweet memory will die

Sometimes I forget why I came here, when it's still and cool like this. The rhythm I live to is changing and it suits me too well. If I don't get out and buy a paper, I forget what day it is. But even if I doze through the small hours, I'm always awake with the birds. Each morning I have a new sunrise and their song.

There are lots of birds in the city: hedgehogs and a sharp, running fox. I never knew that. But then they're not the animal I'm after.

You'd think he would have come by now.

Three, four days, nights too, and not a sign. Not a blink. It makes me tense, just sitting like this, expecting to see his face. He has a flat and featureless face. In my head I used to call him Elmer, after Elmer Fudd. You know? He had that kind of face. He'll still have it, I suppose. That means I can be sure I'll know him when he comes. I believe I will know him. That's something to be glad of.

This is a bad place. The headlamps rock across me and away. They make it seem very open in here and then very closed and they show you that this is a bad place.

We used to live here, Elmer and me, but now it's changed. Now it isn't safe to be alone. At night, if you're alone and walking, then you must be drunk, or stupid, or else you've got no choice because here is your home. I'm saying that even a man would not be safe here and that I can only stay because I can sit in the car and if something unpleasant develops, I simply drive away. This is a place you drive through to get at the city, or to leave it and go near the country and the good place where you live. This is a place you drive through.

Maybe that's why Elmer stays here. I know I can only take jobs where I travel, because now I can't be still. He can't afford to travel, not Elmer, not now, so perhaps by living here, he can feel the roads around him moving and imagine that he's moving too. Maybe he needs that. I don't know.

Thinking about Elmer. I feel like doing that. It's very easy. I've done it before.

Our man.

The man we're after.

Elmer Fudd.

I don't know when he was born, but once he had been, they christened him Joseph McKean. This meant that the boys at his work could call him Joe, when he grew up. One Saturday morning, some time after his birth, Joseph McKean married Margaret Brown, at that time nineteen weeks pregnant, but discretely so. At Somebody's Memorial Church. The far side of town.

Margaret looked very pretty, by the way. I've seen the picture. She wore white; the silk white of fresh snow in the morning, but her eyes, though bright, were lowered. She blushed. Her hair was a stiff, blurred dome of honey twists and laquer. I remember it as a soft, sweet thing, not hard and ugly, like that.

Three weeks short of the anticipated date, at 2.35 am, the young Mrs McKean gave birth to a female child.

Me.

I have never imagined the father was anyone other than Joseph McKean.

But this hasn't described him, this hasn't told us what he's like. My father, for example, always undressed in the wardrobe, out of shame. A singular habit, I haven't encountered since. Every Summer, we would go away together. To

One room.

Double bed.
Single bed.
Sink.
and naturally a
Wardrobe.

And every night and morning, he would climb into the wardrobe and shut the door. I failed to understand why he did this. He would merely exchange his outdoor shirt and trousers for pyjama trousers and top. Vest, socks and underpants would always remain beneath. When these were changed, I never knew.

My mother, I noticed, took all this for granted, as we undressed together outside, in the silent room. When I was older and had learned to listen, I would lie awake at home and hear the door of their wardrobe open and shut. The tiny whisper of springs, as he slipped into bed.

Elmer was away a lot, just then. His work. And my mother shaped her days around his absence. He was carefully prepared for, expected, and whenever she heard the telephone, she would run. She didn't want to make him wait. When she was sure it was him, her voice would slowly empty into something frail and grey. Then she would come to find me with that awful smile.

I think we'll just read tonight, Sweetie. No television, eh? I'm getting a sore head. Oh yes, and Daddy's coming home soon. That'll be nice.

I remember the first time he hit her. The sound of their feet through the ceiling, her body when it fell and then the silence and then the noise. The blow and the hurt from the blow. Almost together, but not quite.

No. I don't remember that. Not a single part of that. I'm telling lies. I can hardly remember my mother at all. You know what she is to me? The woman with the lacquered honey hairstyle in the picture, her forehead out of focus, but clear eyes. Oh, I do have little bits of her from holidays and special times. A Christmas mother, holding a puppet, so that I'd see how it worked. I know that when she sent me to my first day at school, she seemed much more scared than I did. That was the first time I ever felt brave, or lonely, or grown up. But just when I was getting used to being there; the clothes and the rules and the smells; she died. I always wished she could have waited until I was less preoccupied.

The piece about the wardrobe, though, that was true. Only most of the time, it happened when my mother was already gone and I was alone. Alone with Elmer. I don't have to tell lies about him. There were real things I didn't like.

There was the day when I saw him standing in my bedroom window and looking down. What he saw was 1969 on a rainy afternoon, a girl leaving his house with her bag and his umbrella. She was angry, you could see it in her walk.

I saw the same girl last Tuesday. She's why I'm here.

Shall I tell you the way she looked then, or the way that she looks just now? The way that Elmer might have seen her, if he'd ever imagined what was ahead?

Now. I can only remember now.

So. Let us look at her walking, just over the way from me, carrier bag in one hand and leaning on a pram. No, a pushchair, not a pram, and a child in it, crying and waving his head. She pushes the chair in front of her, lets it take some of her weight, and he cries. Loud. People look back at the two of them when they've passed.

Starting from the ground, she wears five inch, white stilletos with mud and pieces of grass dried to the heels. A thin, gold chain rests on the bone of her ankle and then white, cotton trousers begin, mid way along her calf. The trousers are loose until they reach her hips, her arse. The appropriate phrase at this point being.

Like two live rabbits in a sack.

Hanging off the back end of a truck.

And fighting.

No offence, but if we were friends I would have told her that. About the triangle of her knickers showing through, about acting her age and self respect and did somebody tell her they liked her like that? With the tiny, lime green T-shirt top? It showed how thin her back was and pale, like her arms.

I never thought, she must have been cold. On a day like that. No coat.

She turns her head towards me, maybe thinking of crossing the road, and you can see the care she's taken with her makeup. Then you see the bruise. It starts a progression in your head.

From the time before it happened, to the hand against her face, to the way the people stare this morning and her child crying and crying in the street.

I followed her here and asked questions.

Yes, this is where she lives; her and her man. Mr McKean? Well, he's a short, a round kind of man and he generally wears a hat, because he's baldie.

That part made me laugh. He was only thinning before. Now he's completely bald. Just like Elmer Fudd.

I cannot understand why she's stayed with him. We're talking about years. From 1969, and you know how long that is. Even if he had nothing to do with the mark she's got on her face, I simply cannot imagine what he could possibly offer her. I mean, she must be almost the same age as me .

Back in that grey afternoon, when I saw her first? I had followed her that time, too. I was back to visit Elmer. It was coming up to a birthday, something like that and I would stay for the weekend, because I thought I should. By now, I was living and working away. Not my home yet, just away.

I left the bus stop and turned to go down to the house, a little behind a young woman. I didn't really look at her closely, I was paying more attention to the street. It seemed just a little more faded, a little more worn than before and was that because of the way that I felt, or because I had seen it last in the Spring and this was Autumn come again? I didn't know.

She was two or three hundred yards ahead when I saw her open our garden gate and walk up our garden path to our door, open it with her key. I carried on past, checked the house. It was our house. Then I went to call Elmer from the box at the end of the street. It was working.

Hello Dad.

I told him I'd get a taxi and would be there very soon, then I didn't replace the receiver when he rang off. I held it across my face and I watched. She left the house, five minutes later, slamming the door, with Elmer looking on from my bedroom window. She was angry, you could see it in her walk.

See that boy, there, climbing up the sign for the pelican crossing? Same thing every night. Straight up. One time, he'll get to the top. I've seen him almost make it. You look and then, on his way down, he presses the button and lights the white light. It says WAIT. He turns on the light where he's standing and another one flicks up opposite. Three roads intersect there, so behind him and beside him there are lights, echoing lights, whispering WAIT to one another, across the empty streets. This boy worries me. He should be in bed.

The tree this car is under, it's a beech. Wher I lived here last, this road was lined with trees, but now this is the only one and it's a beech. You can tell because we're back to Autumn and it's time for the beechmast to fall. Do you hear it? It falls on the pavement and the tarmac and when it bounces, you can hear. It comes on the roof above us and it sounds like the start of rain. I've been here, listening, when everything else has stopped and now I recognise the sound of beechmast when it falls

Seeing my Father matters enough for me to have waited this long.

Can you imagine the life with my Father? I think of it and, of course, the way his mind worked seems entirely familiar now. Current and comfortable. Our moral and spiritual betters, our leading lights, the dispensers of health and the bakers of daily bread, all follow my Father's humble path. Except it's a metalled road now, and it's growing. I don't know why I bothered to leave him, his influence has spread around and before me until you can't hear a word in parliament for the swinging of the wardrobe doors. You can't hear yourself think. I am at home again with all that Elmer taught me at my side.

I learned well: there are some things, like yourself, that can be altered and some things, like sex and cancer, you have to ignore. But the wrong kinds of people and the wrong alterations made; all you can do with them is hate. I am a good hater. I find it easy.

That was what my Father made me do. People say that you are what your parents make you. I say that you are what your parents make you do. Elmer made me hate and now I am tired of hating and now I am here to see him and put that right. My change of life. I should have done it years ago, but I thought that I'd left him behind when I ran away.

Those were the days, the days in '69, when people could still run away. In a town about fifty miles south of here, now a little depressed, I got myself a job and then a bedsit. Very nice. The deal was the same as in all of these places: no visitors, drugs or drink and pay up a week in advance. I felt at home.

But there were always the little parties with the bottles wrapped in paper the following day. We threw them away with the stale dowps in different litter bins. Sometimes there were even joints. Nothing heavy, just something a wee bit exciting that made you laugh. I remember a skinny blonde girl once, sitting in a corner, watching her hands and laughing, kissing them and laughing again. Also at a couple of parties there was Paul.

Maybe you can imagine the life with Elmer, but you can't imagine this. All the love. Like two o'clock in the morning and Paul wakes me up. He lets himself in with the key I had cut and I hear him in my sleep, wake without being frightened and he's there. There's rain outside, it's cold in his hair. His hands are cold, even his stomach, under his shirt and when I hold him I can feel him smile. We're a nice surprise for each other. We smile and light the dark.

Wouldn't you fight for that? Wouldn't you need it and use it to drive out all the hate? If you were me?

The last time I visited Elmer, even then, I was happy. Even there. I was pregnant. Not showing, but achey and always hungry, always pissing, tired. Elmer had married the girl, Leslie, and we talked for a bit about nothing. I think she guessed how I was, but she never said and I wasn't telling, so my Father never knew he had a grandson. He doesn't now.

We called the baby Sandy, then got married. We wanted to do that. We were going to be more married than anyone, ever before. We were going to redefine it.

Paul and I both still had to work. I had a minder in and just did mornings, but he stayed away all day. We tried to get Sandy used to sleeping early and still keep our evenings free to talk, but it didn't work out. Something always happened, interrupted, and I couldn't remember how to give Paul what he wanted any more. I wished he wouldn't ask. What it was I wanted, I didn't know.

Sometimes I would look at Sandy and there were bits of Paul shining through in him and good bits of me and it made what we were together seem much better. I could watch Paul, watching him, and know that he thought the same, but most of the time, we didn't have a chance to think. Sandy kept us too busy, wanting things and breaking things. He broke us.

It would have come in any case, of course, he only made it faster. There were times when I thought he meant it, but they passed. It wasn't Sandy's fault. He was a good boy; I hope he still is. Paul and I postponed our arguments until Sandy was safely delivered, but once that was over, we wheeled them back again. We hadn't forgotten a word.

It would happen, usually quite late, with Sandy sleeping, or at least packed off to bed, and something would spring things all open again and then we would have to begin. Everything we said would be circular, perfect with repetition, meaningless and hurtful and slowly grinding in. In the end, we hardly recognised each other, or ourselves, and we found it very difficult to stop.

We could tire each other out in the beginning, but our stamina increased. Later, we tried to fuck it away and that worked for a while, but, finally, we couldn't break away. We had to make it hurt before it would go.

I was the one who started that. I hit Paul. I didn't want him near me, so I kicked him and he kicked me back. We slept in each other's arms that night, frightened and sharing this new thing together: the first time we'd come to blows. In the morning, I had bruises on my shoulders and my back. He had tender ribs. It wasn't much; the marks were almost signs of love. We were quiet for nearly a fortnight, then watchful, but gentle and close. When the hitting came again, it was different and I think you might say cold.

One Sunday afternoon, just before dinner, I was upstairs on our bed. I'd come up for a nap and now I was still sleepy, but thinking of getting up. I heard Paul come in, quite softly, and a key turn in the door. We never used to lock that door, not even because of Sandy. I didn't know it had a key. But Paul must have looked and found it, intending to do what he did. What happened when he turned the key and locked us in.

I felt his weight dip and move on the bed and I turned to see him, opened my eyes. It felt good to roll over, expecting him. It always did.

It's funny, all the time it happened I thought of Sandy. I didn't want him to hear us. I didn't want him to know. He

59

would have heard me falling, he would have heard the body, the feet, the head, but he didn't hear my voice. I never made a sound that might worry him.

Paul was quiet, too. There was only the noise inside when he hit me and the sound it made outside, in the room. The sound he would listen to. Each time, he gave a short, little breath, no more. I bit him and he gave a little breath, I felt him in me and he gave a little breath, he came and then he gave a little breath.

When he left and I heard the front door close behind him, there was no sound at all, just a thick, dizzy silence you could taste.

Wind the window down and it's silent here, too. We're in the pause before the false dawn arrives and then a train pours along beside the river and it's broken. The moment's away.

Sandy will be here, somewhere, nearly grown to be a man. He was a good boy, nice looking, appealing to adoptive parents. He won't have stayed long in a home. We only said we couldn't cope for a while and asked if they could help us out. There were things I thought he shouldn't have to see. They helped us out and took him, but I never got him back.

He'll have gone to good people. I know that.

I wish I could picture him happy and older, with good people, but I can only see him standing at the bottom of the stairs, waiting for me to come down, that afternoon. I saw in his face, that he'd heard too much. I tried to hurry and held out my arms and he stared at me and then he ran. He looked at me as if I'd told him lies and now he knew it and then ran to the sofa in the sitting room and fell there, crying, hunched up. I couldn't uncurl him. I had to kneel and hold him like that.

He had his own smell, Sandy, his exact own smell. The same when he was sleeping and you kissed him goodnight, the same when you dried him after baths, the same when I held him against me, felt his shoulders tight and heard him cry. He would still have that.

Someday I might stand beside him, perhaps in a lift, or a shop, and I would know.

Soon I have to drive away. There's a place that isn't far from here where they cook a good breakfast. I walk about there, use their toilet and have a wash. This is Thursday, very early on a

60

Thursday and by Monday I have to be miles away, back at work. It could be months before I'm here again; more than a year; and by then I could have lost him for good. Even now, while I'm away, Elmer could come and go and there'd be no trace. I might have missed him already, twenty, fifty, a hundred times.

The curious thing is, I no longer care.

The role of notable silences in Scottish history

I find it very hard to tell the truth. Why this should be the case, I do not know. I was brought up quite respectably in a God fearing home and went to a school where prunes and haggis walked hand in hand with Christian fortitude. A lapsed Methodist lay-preacher, my mother did her best and my father was a man who was frequently and visibly frightened of God. Still, I find it very hard to tell the truth.

Worse than this, I have discovered that, beyond a certain point, nobody really cares much if you lie. And I do lie. I can be honest with you. I can tell you that I do not tell the truth. I can also say that no one notices.

In my work, I am intended to collect true things and write them down for the convenience of others. I am meant to read books, suck their insides out, and give them to people who don't read books. Because I'm here to do it for them. I turn numbers into graphs, graphs into conclusions and conclusions into numbers again. I like that; it's very neat. And the numbers you get at the end are always different from the ones you had to start with. That's a constant source of satisfaction.

I enjoy my work, it is clean and varied, it pays a good wage. Sadly, it is also a constant temptation. Time and again, it presents the perfect opportunity to lie. It begs you to lie. It also repeatedly proves beyond all shadow of a doubt that nothing is less believable than the truth.

My researches have discovered the author who pelted his wife with boiled potatoes at least once a month, the infamous Yorkshire maggot boom and at least one woman with two pairs of legs and these things are true things, made up of verifiable fact. The eminent sex therapist's father did indeed attempt a fraudulent insurance claim by standing up to his waist in a duck pond and inducing a fatal dose of pneumonia. There is nothing I can say against it. All of this is true and must be accepted unless I choose to imagine that generations of people like myself have simply been making things up.

This is, of course, quite possible, but also very difficult to prove. Even if such individuals left a record of their crimes against the truth, we couldn't believe them. They wouldn't be the kind of people we could trust.

Now while I'm working, I try not to think about the truth and concentrate my full attention on the words instead. Words just say what you want them to; they don't know any better. We get on very well together, even in the dusty mornings when all we have to amuse ourselves are maps and historical geography

GLEN FLASPOG

The Glen's most notable feature is a series of spectacular falls, descending from twelve hundred feet above the valley floor.

All cascades, the Grand McIver, the Evil Red McIver and the Torrent of the Weeping Mother's have now been without water for several centuries; in memory, it is said, of the dreadful Massacre of the McIvers, perpetrated by the Evil Red McIver upon his own kinsmen.

Other tales of more ancient origin suggest that the falls have, in fact, never run with water, except in seasons of unique precipitation, and that their name derives from an elaborate and now forgotten practical joke.

The Evil Red McIver's band of One Hundred Renegades was famed for an unswerving loyalty to its chief. Any member of The Band would willingly jump from the top of the Falls of McIver to his death, at the merest nod of his leader's head.

The last surviving member of The Band expired in just such a fashion, the Evil Black McIver, his companion in the descent. Later observers have been unable to determine whether this final act constituted desperate murder, or a suicide pact.

A small cairn at the foot of the Falls marks the spot.

None of this is true, of course, but it is far more interesting than a brown and green glen with rocky grey bits and a couple of sheep. Had far-sighted landlords not cleared the ground of all its people centuries ago, the place would probably look like Castlemilk. Everything relies on chance, on coincidence. And there's no point being Scottish if you can't make up your past as you go along.

Everyone else does.

But here is a thing I do know to be true, because it has happened to me. Go into any place where history is stored and listen. Hold your breath. Hear how still it is. Librarians and archivists will keep their visitors quiet, but this particular silence has nothing to do with them. It runs through buzzing computer rooms and waits in busy record offices, it is always there. It is the sound of nothingness. It is the huge, invisible, silent roar of all the people who are too small to record. They disappear and leave the past inhabited only by murderers and prodigies and saints.

At first the sound is almost soothing, like the wash of a tender sea. Then you begin to consider that only a lifetime from now, you will be part of that silence and nothing more. I don't like that. It makes what I do seem pointless.

Let us put it like this.

Why should I write about people when most of the people can never be written about because they have completely disappeared? Not a National Insurance number, not hairs caught in a comb. They're gone.

And look at the people I do have to write about. The space I have to give them is always rationed by somebody else. I can only use the number of words I am given in each request. Sometimes I have to squeeze a figure of genuine stature and worth into the space of two hundred and fifty words. Equally, I might get five thousand for some syphillitic bampot whose only real achievement was a speedy and popular death. Under these circumstances, it can only be healthy for me to start making things up.

At the moment, I am working for the Local Passenger Transport Executive. They want me to say what they already think about buses.

Buses are the transport of the poor, trains being rendered inflexible by their rails, cars improbable by their expense and taxis impossible by their extravagant fares and their disinclination to make for destinations the poor might choose. Therefore, if the poor are not walking, they have probably taken the bus.

There are, furthermore, many persons among the poor who are possessed of a concessionary pass. By this means, those who are old, stupid, crippled, deformed or otherwise unfit may travel cheaply and frequently to excess. They are joined by those who neither work nor want in cut price jaunts and pleasurable escapades. Those rendered insensible by drink may find in any bus an audience for sentimental ballads, a steadying hand, a patient ear, directions to any location, a corner to sleep in and a floor on which to deposit their most recent meal.

Unwary travellers from other lands, not fully acquainted with our language may inadvertently happen to board a bus. Unaware of the bus's true nature they will mistake both their fare and their way and be submitted to untold indignities en route while their final destination will be constantly in doubt. Such international incidents cannot help but usher in a new age of disharmony between nations.

The influence of queueing upon the impressionable minds of the poor has already been well proven. The persistent and prolonged queueing, so much a part of life in Eastern Europe has led to recent unrest in Poland, Bulgaria, Hungary, Czechoslovakia and even Mother Russia herself. Accustomed to the presence of others in large, slow moving queues, groups begin to experiment, forming crowds and other large assemblies, before coming together in bloodthirsty, riotous mobs. The Berlin

Wall was defeated, not by democracy, but by queues.

The poor of this country are already much oppressed by queueing at offices of Housing, Post and Dole and frequent participation in bus queues could well be the final straw that turns the worm. As buses cannot function without stops and stops cannot function without queues and queues are the immediate precursors of bloody revolution and wholesale revolt it may be said, quite reasonably, that all buses are a threat to society.

The significance of request stops will be dealt with in more detail below.

It should also be borne in mind that buses are the very agents which carry the poor from their areas of seclusion into the broad streets and flowered avenues to which they can never aspire. From the lofty vantage point provided by the upper deck, how many pairs of eyes may look into rooms furnished with unimaginable, subtlety and taste? How many times can these people glimpse environmental art, cosmopolitan piazzas and telephone boxes with doors and sides, before they will want them, too?

Just as the trenches at Ypres and Passchendale brought together the player and the gentleman with unforeseen results; so the bus may be responsible for irreversible damage to the very order and serenity on which our lives are based.

We must therefore conclude that buses, far from being a necessary evil, are a cancer, gnawing the roots of all we hold most dear. The impact of the Sunday service remains too horrible to contemplate.

They liked that. They called it well balanced and exhaustively researched.

Some assignments can be absorbing, even obsessional, but I find it aids clear thinking to have an outside interest or two. I do, in fact, have two. When I am out in the city, I enjoy walking and when I am at home, I read. I used to like murder mysteries, but now I prefer historical romance.

When I walk I see a wonderful city, built in blocks like Boston or New York. This makes it very inviting and hard to get lost in, because its shape is governed by a grid. There are also times, especially in winter, when the sky is solid blue, the sunlight rich and low and the city becomes beautiful. Even where there are chip shops with metal shutters and the homes have putrefied around their tenants; even where there are beggars, really beggars, at the feet of each refurbished edifice, the light that falls here makes it beautiful. This is a city where ugly things happen under a beautiful light.

I was out walking quite recently, just clearing my head in the kind of clean afternoon a frost will leave. I went up Blythswood Street which crosses St Vincent Street and then West George Street and leads into a corner of Blythswood Square. I walked around the square and into West George Street again and into Pitt Street, where the policemen live, along and into St Vincent Street and back into Blythswood Street. Then down.

That's the way the grid works, if you follow it, you can't go wrong. It looks after you.

On my walk I noticed two things, which stayed in my mind. In Blythswood Square, I passed the house of Madeleine Smith. It's Number Seven. I stood by the railings her lover once reached through to take the poisoned cocoa she offered him. I looked at the brass nameplate which said MADELEINE SMITH HOUSE and then I went on. In West George Street, the pavement hums beneath your feet. You pass yellow signs which show a man being struck by lightning, and words that say KEEP OUT and DANGER OF DEATH. Behind the folding metal doors, there are two hundred and seventy five thousand volts, it tells you that, too, and you can feel them in the air and under your feet. All that power is picking away at the mortar between the bricks and leaking out. You wonder if Madeleine's sweetheart felt something of the same strange agitation as he stood at the railings and held out his hand for the cup.

This city makes you think like that. The roads come together, cross and go on and little strands of history follow them. In some places, many lines will cross: what has been, what is and what will be and you can walk from one coincidence to another, not step on a crack. It's like strolling across a book, something big and Victorian with plenty of plots. It makes you wonder who's reading you.

Sitting above my own books I find lines of coincidence there, too. You could almost believe that some things were meant to happen. Mackintosh is bound to invent the raincoat, Wallace has to be captured and taken to Smithfield for slaughter, it is inevitable that Sandwich will discover the piece and jam. The evidence points to only one conclusion in every case.

It's the same with crime, especially murder. People enter a line of coincidence and follow it to the end. There is more than a touch of predestination about it. The chances domino against them; wrong time, wrong place, open window, unlucky acquaintance, excess of trust and suddenly they are half of something unanticipated. And then they are silence.

I've read up on the subject, seen the evidence.

Killing Time: Seven centuries of Scottish slaughter by Rosamund Lundquist (Flaspog Press, £25.99)

'If you prick us do we not bleed? If you poison us do we not die?' So begins Rosamund Lundquist's latest excursion into Scots pathology. What parallels might be drawn between a Viennese moneylender and a Scottish cadaver are never made clear, but Ms Lundquist forges ahead in characteristically fulsome style with any weakness in her prose more than compensated for by a wealth of contemporary engravings, woodcuts and photographs. Much use is made of that hardy standby, the coroner's report, while frequent exhumations and dissections give the book its distinctive flavour.

The overall unity of Ms Lundquist's conception is made obvious from the outset by *Killing Time*'s inspired cover illustration, featuring details from a notable Scottish post mortem. More disturbing, is the customary author's photograph, showing Ms Lundquist on a favourite walk through Twechar cemetery. The biographical details below it are what we have come to expect from a woman whose date of birth is as much in doubt as the year of her parent's wedding and whose only real connection with tertiary education is furnished by persistent liaisons with local undergraduates.

Terse, compelling and at times rather poorly proof read, Ms Lunquist's patient researches pack over 8,000 pages with murders wholesale and domestic, inadvertant and perverse.

Readers may question some of Lundquist's editorial decisions; Caligula's excesses, for example, are included because of his rumoured fondness for the Sunday Post; and I must number myself among those who find this a somewhat tenuous Scottish connection. Attila the Hun's penchant for potato scones would have made him a much stronger candidate for inclusion.

Not withstanding its many defects and Rosamund Lundquist's unconventional lifestyle, *Killing Time* makes a satisfying, easy read. Its chapter, especially for children, *Playing Dead*, is both funny and informative.

No doubt this latest volume will join the distinguished ranks of Scottish Classic Literature, alongside *Bonnie Charlie's Glasgow Cookbook* and *Fish of the Outer Hebrides*.

People like to read about murders; they find them comforting. You place the facts before them, polite but frank, and you ease the fear and mystery out of death. You are simply showing them a problem which you solve. It's easy.

When I research a murder, it's sometimes for other people and sometime for myself. If it's for other people, I work with books, but if it's for myself, I work with people. Anyone can do it.

Perhaps you go into a pub for an orange juice and lemonade one night. You tuck yourself up in a corner and keep very quiet the way that a solitary lady always should. Maybe there's a record on the jukebox that you know and you're singing along with the verse. You look over to the bar and there you have him: his lips mouthing the shapes you know your mouth is making and both of you singing with someone else's voice. Both of you look away because you have to, both of you stop singing, almost without noticing. Not long after, he goes outside.

It isn't hard for a woman to follow a man. They don't expect it, you're not a threat. And you disappear and they don't see you and you start to follow them again.

If I know where somebody lives, I can find out their name, their telephone number, their job, where they go and when they go there, whether they buy *The Sun* or *The Angling Times*. I can walk up the stairs in their close and look down on their doorway and I can feel them breathe.

I assume this is what murderers often do.

This harmless pastime means I can make the most of both my hobbies. I get to read; telephone directories, registers for Poll Tax, even letters and I get to walk. All over the city.

I have no sinister intention, please believe me. None at all. I simply pick men and sometimes women, who are in no way notable, and when I know all about them, I write their obituary.

I have a whole book of them; death notices. I have to imagine the way they might die, I have to make that up, but everything else I put down is the absolute truth. In this respect, my anthology is unique. Conventional reports are wholly truthful when they deal with the manner of death and only begin to lie when they look at the life.

And I should know, after all. I do know about lies.

Which is perhaps why I like this city so much and to walk in it, especially at night, when the dark bolts out of closes and children gather to stalk the buses and stone them to death. The city knows about lies, too. It makes them and loves them and forgets they were never the truth.

I once hunted a man, collected his life, enquired at his place of employment and found him staring up at me from behind a small desk. He had been reading a Statistical Account of Dundee and District. We smiled and took our glasses off.

There followed a profitable series of collaborative endeavours.

We went out together in the city dark. In the dark it relaxes a little and loses its sense of time, things blur. We felt Highland mutineers running and running, solemn English soldiers, patrolling a January bridge and the hard shot of muskets, tapping at the bodies of discontented men and going in and going in. The street full of weavers, lying still. Murderers hang, tramways open, exhibitions are held and mothers give birth to children of great importance. And always there are voices, of all kinds, alone and singing or harsh above the heads of the crowds. There are all kinds of crowd.

Although I often work without any reference to notes, my companion was constantly writing, recording, scribbling on a variety of pads. As we travelled together, he compiled our list of lies. We found lies about ships, the weather, trains, commu-

70

nal toilets, drink, pies, bridies, comedians, drunks, singers, happiness, tea shops, culture, blueprints, socialists, hunger, anger, clay, houses, capitalists, painters, hogmanay and Irn Bru.

In my home, away from the pavements and the railway lines, we made other lists of notable features. The spark of blue inside the lightswitch, the growth and removal of dust, the differences of breath and skin. His notebooks fill two shoe boxes under my bed.

He was murdered by accident, not design. He was stabbed by a stranger in a bar. Earlier there had been fighting and one of the stranger's friends had been slashed with a glass. Because the stranger believed in lies about blood loyalty and city violence, he came to the pub to make them true. He walked straight in, quite quickly, and stabbed my friend. My friend had chosen to stand in the wrong place.

With stomach wounds the knife should be left in position, so that the blade can seal what it has severed. If this procedure is not followed, there may be a danger of death. My friend wished to explain this, but only found the words to say it in the ambulance where he died. There were two wounds. Perhaps the stranger had tried to replace his knife.

Because I have his notebooks, my friend has not disappeared, he isn't silent. I have his evidence. There are newspaper clippings, too, about his murder, but none of them mention what we were together. My house is full of the roaring of us together, like the silence after loud music has been stopped. Sometimes I wake and wonder if I made him up and I'm afraid to look for the boxes under the bed. I dream badly.

I should, perhaps, record our details. I should immortalise our city's strange effects. It is in the habit of murdering. Part of its construction is made for killing. People have built it like that; fatal, but disinterested, like a gun. Some of us live in the barrel of the gun and some of us do not. And some of us describe the mechanism and remind everyone how beautiful it is.

Our city and us inside it and me inside us. I should write descriptions of them all, but everyone knows I lie too much, so who would believe me. I wouldn't believe myself. And it's past the time for saying, anything about it now. It's too recent for history and too old to be news. Someone else will find it later, someone like me. They'll take us out and write us down. My only contribution on the subject is already here: the obituary I wrote him before we first met. It is inaccurate.

The high walk

He was thinking of the flat and Partickhill. Incredible. All this way he'd come and the view was like the Scotland you would dream of from abroad, but here he stood and thought of Partickhill.

As it would be in the winter time, at evening, he saw it like that. He would be standing at the top of a road, maybe Gardner Street, and looking down at the dark and the lights of Partick. You knew it was mostly houses and people and shops, but it never looked like that; not at night. To him, it always seemed like a valley full of coals down there. There were lines and patterns of lights, all sparkling white and orange and roping through an irregular dark like random fire. Corners and faces of buildings, lit in slivers, suggested nothing at all, or nothing that he wanted to consider. They were a dim threat, tapping away, like the long hands of the cranes and, beyond them, the invisible river. The dark thought of a river.

He was annoyed with himself for remembering all of that now.

He looked at Annie, a wee bit ahead on the track and pausing again. She was loving it here. It was great; like having a child with you, to be surprised at things. She must have forgotten they were up here for a purpose, that there were reasons why they'd come. He could tell from the line of her back she was just relaxed and looking at the view. That morning she'd washed her hair in the hostel and now it was flying up, even in this little breeze. You could see that she wasn't pure blonde, that there was red in there, too. She looped the hair round behind her ears and it fluttered away again. She should tie it back, or up. He had suggested it.

Annie? Anne?

Mmm? Come and see. Look at them all down there.

On the near side of the glen, a long line of figures straggled down to the river: dots of blue and black and brilliant red, moving slowly on. A dog barked from somewhere, but they couldn't see it.

If we don't hurry up, we'll not make the cairn for lunch.

That would snap her out of it. She did get dreamy sometimes. Would that matter?

No, it wouldn't matter. But we'll have to stop when we reach it, in any case. Just wait until you see the view from there, Annie. There's a whole, new glen opens out on the other side. And a loch. We'll have to stop and look. I'll bet I won't get you away.

Well, come on then. Are there deer here?

Oh, I should think so. I haven't been looking for tracks. There should be deer.

She smiled one of her funny, wee smiles and started up the track. It surprised him how lightly she walked. Her boots were substantial: nice, but quite a weight: and yet she drew further and further ahead, effortless and neat. As if she was strolling in trainers. And you couldn't hear one step. He always seemed to clump, he couldn't help it.

I wonder if they'll find her.

So, she hadn't forgotten that. He told her not to worry. There was no need.

I'm not worried. I just wondered if they will. In time, I mean.

He regretted having told her now. He should have known it might pray on her mind. A young girl, six or seven, had disappeared from her parent's car. They'd been parked down near the river yesterday, just off the road, and they'd gone for a walk, while the girl slept in the car. She must have woken and gone to look for them. She must have got lost.

He did feel sympathetic. He thought he'd seen the father,

that morning, with the police. Him, or somebody else, looking taut and pale. But it seemed so stupid, just to go away and leave a child. Near water, too. They'd been dragging the river since dawn. No luck yet.

Annie had turned from the track. She was peering down off the bank and into the firs, intent. He expected she'd seen a rabbit tail, blinking away. Certainly not a deer.

There's a squirrel in there, I saw it.

Grey?

No, a red one. That kind of Irish Setter red. I've never seen one before.

A red squirrel?

Yes, only for a moment. They're very small, aren't they?

I couldn't say. It was maybe a small one you saw. They're not big, though. No. Not even as big as a cat, more like a kitten.

I'm glad I came.

Yes, so am I.

It's nice to be able to see things with someone else there. You know; to be there and see them, too.

It's nice to be able to see things with you, Anne. Annie...

She jumped down off the bank, walked on and he couldn't think of something else to say.

He wanted to ask her why she came, what did she want? The same things as before? Do you want a fuck, do you want your hole, or are you just along as an observer? Or please, will you tell me what happened, after I went away? What did you do? Apart from taking frigid lessons?

Sometimes, he couldn't sleep for wanting to know what happened, what she'd done. He knew it wasn't likely he would ask her. Not out loud. There were other times when it seemed he should leave himself guessing, because you could always change your guess. And, whatever the answer was, it would always be there, ready for when he might ask. She wouldn't forget. She was keeping it all inside: you could see it at the back of that funny, wee smile.

There were things he wouldn't forget. He was sure of that.

August, a sky bruised and dusty with heat; everything sleepy, or ripe and the three of them, all together. It wasn't possible to forget. They had sat on the steps at the mouth of the close, like a Marzaroli picture of a tenement family. They had been a

75

family. Annie and him and their mutual friend, Marie. The Family

It had been a good idea – Annie's, he thought. They had all just graduated and found that their lives had lost their familiar shape. There was nothing else to learn, or at least, no way to prove that you had learned it. No way that they could think of, yet. And they wrote away for jobs they couldn't imagine and worried about their overdrafts. So it was sensible to find a flat together, the three of them, to share expenses and just be around, if somebody needed to talk. They were scared and they could hear their future coming.

Annie and he had been sleeping together for something like six months by then. Or rather, they'd slept together before that, or done things together and then afterwards slept apart. But this domestic stuff, this last thing at night and first thing in the morning, having her there, was a more recent situation. After the something like six months he still wasn't altogether used to it. But it was very nice and, for a while, very horny indeed.

Not that they hadn't needed Marie there, too. She was someone for them to mother and father, once in a while, or someone to run and hide with, whenever they wanted to. She seemed to enjoy the responsibility. In the same way, she enjoyed being far and away the best cook and, if she was slightly unattractive, she was also funny and sensible and there was something about her hidden, that told you she would bloom late. He presumed she was somewhere now, a full grown success, making the most of surprisingly lovely legs.

That hurt. Even now that hurt. Such a tiny thought about Marie and still it could hurt. Because he had been there, with those pale, surprising legs, the blue of the blue veins at her hip bones and the curly, twirly, gingery hair, much more personal and friendly than the straight cut brown on her head. He had done that. Awful. Not awful that way, just an awful thing to do. And he'd done it without even understanding why, so that he felt he'd betrayed himself as much as Marie. And Annie, naturally.

Anne had found them, of course. They were there on the sofa when she came in, which always seemed much more awful than if she'd found them together in bed. He could imagine what she'd seen and how cheap it looked.

It was the first and only time he'd touched Marie like that and he'd delayed so long the urge had almost faded. It was almost too late to be possible. He didn't quite know why they'd waited. It had been in the air for days, in one form or another. They could have done it and had it over before Annie came back that night, but they had waited. He thought now they might have been hoping she would be early getting home and they wouldn't have to go through with it at all.

Marie had pulled her skirt down in silence and walked through to the kitchen where she made a pot of tea. She came back through the sitting room with the tray and out along the corridor to her room. They heard her lock her door.

He remembered he'd wanted to wash himself before he had to speak to Anne. He didn't want to be near her, knowing his prick would smell of Marie: that all of him would. He didn't want to insult her like that. But then Anne sat beside him, so fast it seemed her legs might have given way and he never had time to do anything but stay where he was on the sofa which also smelt of Marie.

Anne was very close to him. Close enough to kiss. He couldn't imagine they wouldn't touch, just by accident. Or if one of them drew in too deep a breath. But Anne was very careful about that. She kept herself still and small and somehow hard and, when she spoke, the words came from far away.

I was, I would have told you this anyway. I wanted to tell you. I hoped you might want to know. About me. And I'll tell you, anyway. I know you don't care, but I'll tell you. I don't care either.

You listen. You just, you listen.

When I was young. I slept in a room I don't even remember now – I only remember the brown stain on the wall. That's how young I was. How long ago. My father and mother went out, this one night. This one night I'll tell you about. And my mother said goodnight to me and she kissed my head and she told me there was someone who was going to come in and keep an eye on me. Not to worry. If I needed anything, just shout. That's not important, what's important is, I slept. I cooried in and it took me a while to settle, but in the end I went to sleep.

I was still asleep when my parents came back. When they walked by the wall at the far end of the street and all the way back, my father beat my mother's head against the bricks. Listen to it. Footsteps along the pavement and her head against the bricks.

My mother knew to keep her mouth shut when they got in. So she wouldn't embarrass the neighbour who'd sat with her child, so she wouldn't hear her name going round the closes. I didn't hear them both, carefully wishing the woman goodnight. I didn't hear the scramble once they shut the door. I didn't hear my own mother's head going on and off a wall again.

He liked to do that to her. That was his trick. On the wall and off the wall. Good trick. They came right into my room like that and my father told my mother she could go if she fucking wanted, but I wouldn't want to go, too.

I didn't hear.

I was asleep when she lifted me up and asked me questions I still don't know. He told her I didn't love her, that I didn't want to go. He didn't say I was only sleeping and couldn't hear.

What would you have told her? What would you have done? Don't worry, it doesn't matter. Don't answer.

I'm saying I couldn't be a child. Between the two of them, I couldn't be a child, but I decided I was going to have one. When I grew up. I was going to give it a wonderful childhood. The best. To make things even.

Christ, I was going to marry you.

Christ. Jesus Christ. I don't want this any more.

Tell me, what would you have called our baby? Eh? Something nice? Shall I guess? Marie? Well, say goodbye to the chance. Right?

Fuck off. Fuck. Off.

She didn't seem at all like that now. Not talking about babies that way and scaring him. She'd been walking out to their room, the room that had then become her room, and he asked her.

Are you pregnant?

She only laughed and asked him if he really wanted to know. He couldn't remember if she'd looked pregnant. Would he have been able to tell? She was the one that insisted on taking the pill. It didn't make sense. She can't have wanted children. And he had asked if she was pregnant. He had done that.

She looked fine today. Her shoulders were back, relaxed, a little weight was away from her hips, just enough, and her eyes had never looked the way they had that night again. As if he was being cursed.

What's wrong?

He realised she was looking at him.

Nothing. I was thinking.

About?

The child. That lost one.

I thought you said not to worry about that. I think somebody took her: from the car. I hope not. It seems like wishing it on her, but I think that'll be what's happened. I'm afraid she's dead.

Well, we're keeping an eye out, up here, like we said we would.

She wouldn't have come up here. Why should she?

But just in case.

I know.

I'm sorry about all this. I mean I'm sorry about it anyway, but I'm sorry about it happening just now.

While we're here, you mean?

While you're here. I come here all the time.

She gave him a look that he didn't quite catch and they crossed the treeline together. All around them now were the shapes of other mountains, intimate, like knees and forearms and bellies under a brown, stained coverlet. The limbs were familiar, some settled under firs, but there was always the feeling that something might happen. A careless movement underneath the sheets.

He had swallowed his pride and called her, hadn't he? He had asked her if she'd like to spend a weekend walking with him. Separate room, no pressure, no fuss. He had sat and listened to her voice and, all the time, the receiver had pressed his ear, reminding him of the bite she'd left him there. It was still tender. Before, it had bled, and now it was just a little painful and it made his stomach jump.

The speed of it all had been astonishing. He'd seen her for the first time in all these years, these years between the awfulness and now, and then he'd called her and they'd almost set a meeting. Then, on the spur of the moment, he'd thought that they ought to go walking instead and now they were here. From nothing up to this inside a month.

It must, he thought, have had something to do with fate. He'd met her again at a party he shouldn't have been at, a housewarming, but Andy had come round to fetch him and he'd gone. He'd stood in a stranger's kitchen, its walls peeled of paper and ready for something new, and filled a glass with water. It had filled and over filled until the water running chill over his fingers made them hurt.

I thought it was you.

She had come to the doorway and waited, looking in.

Anne?

That's right. Are you a friend of Michael's, too?

Not really, no.

I didn't think so. I'll see you again, before you go.

He went back to the sitting room and Andy, who left him with a teacher called Irene. He didn't like her. In the end he went out to look for his coat in the hall. Anne was sitting at the kitchen table with two other women and he didn't think she'd noticed him, but when finally he'd found his coat and was pulling it on, he heard footsteps behind him and turned.

If you're leaving, I'll give you a lift. That is, if you still don't drive.

Her car was nice, a Nissan Something, and she drove it well. He couldn't remember the journey, so probably they didn't speak. She parked by his house, very neatly, and he thought he should kiss her goodbye and perhaps he did lean towards her, he wasn't quite sure. What he was certainly sure of was her mouth, closing over his ear, taking all of his ear and making it hot and wet and surprised.

He had wanted to turn and touch her, to put her hand on his leg, in his lap, but her teeth were pinched round his ear and, when he tried to move, she bit him. Very hard. He bled.

Bye, then.

Mmh?

She turned away again, indicating, checking mirrors, doing driving things.

Goodbye.

Well, will I... I'll call you. Anne?

Did she smile then, or did it only seem that way?

80

That's fine, you do that.

Well. OK.

Bye.

He couldn't think why he'd called her, after that. Or why she'd agreed to come. Almost beside him now, she was different from the night on the sofa and different from the night in the car. She was nice. She smelt nice. Her sweater was off and tied around her waist, her T-shirt showing slim and slightly freckled arms, a light down on the skin. Nice tits; still nice tits. She could be only twenty, twenty-one. There was something a little tight in her face that made her seem slightly older, but she must be twenty-seven by now and she didn't look that.

She didn't look old enough to have ever been pregnant, not old enough for children at all. It was stupid to imagine it.

Was that what she'd said to the doctor; too young? No, she'd never said anything, guess again.

Is that the cairn up there?

Mmm? Oh, aye. Uh hu.

I thought it would be bigger somehow.

Uh hu?

I suppose it only seemed small by comparison – with the mountains. Anne? I was thinking. After this weekend, will I see you again?

Well, you don't live all that far away.

No, I mean, will I see you?

No.

When they came to the cairn he let Annie find the view for herself and sat with his back against the stones and stared at grass. The sky was too blue to look at and, around him, the old heather stalks were weathered to the paleness of bones.

Both of them closed their eyes for a time, felt the sun, red through their lids. In the glen, the lines were still searching for a child who had been lost. So far, nothing found.

Star Dust

The first snow fell tonight; this evening. There's something about it being there, outside; the soft, wavering shadows against the glass. Inside, however you were feeling, as soon as you realise snow is here – the first snow again – you get better, you feel snug.

I wanted to open a window tonight, to put my hand outside into the weather and let the flakes tickle on my palm. In a few hours there will be rain, or sleet, or something and, by morning, what I see will no longer be new. People will no longer walk through a different country, strange and careful, as if they were being watched. I should keep this as it is. I should take a photograph.

Sometimes I am asked to say why I started taking photographs and I tell them because my daughter bought me a television set. If I were younger, that would make them puzzled and they would ask me to explain, but now, of course, they smile because I can't have understood them and then they leave and tell each other I'm confused.

But the truth is that I did start taking pictures when my daughter sent the television set. I had never wanted one – never in my life; books and the films and radio were always enough for me, but still she sent me one, even though I told her not. Didn't I have to stare at one for fifteen years, perhaps longer, and don't I know by now what I do not like? In any case, it came in time for Christmas and in the New Year, it would be company for me.

It was company for someone else because I sold it. The January papers were filled with unwanted gifts and I didn't get the price I might have done. I wasn't worried. The camera that I wanted was quite inexpensive and, even buying film and a cleaning kit, I found I had a deal of money left. Some of this I spent on photography books, because borrowing them from the library wasn't enough and I needed to know about filters and lenses, exposure times and depths of field. I love these words. These words are lovely. They are happening now, they are young words and, because I understand them, part of me can still be happening now and young.

Still, I always buy the TV and Radio Times and study them for Susan's sake, so whenever she phones I can talk about the programmes I don't watch. But she doesn't often ask.

How do I really explain about the photographs? Unless I say that television pictures can't belong to me and can't be a special occasion that could please me like the cinema and so my daughter's offer made me discontented. Or, at best, it made me realise how discontented I was because I have always wanted pictures that would be mine and that would keep a hold of special things. Things like the first snow.

A woman in my position, I know, shouldn't need a camera. All my momentous occasions have happened, apart from my funeral and I won't be taking any pictures there. I haven't even got a family, or loved ones to photograph: Archie's been gone for years, now, and Susan lives in London with a man I hardly know.

London. That doesn't seem fair. While I was younger and fit for it, we never had the money to go there and, even with the money, we couldn't have found the time. We would never have thought. Now travelling is faster and doesn't, I suppose, cost quite so much and certainly I've plenty time, but my health has gone and I couldn't face the journey. I got down twice on my pensioner's card and it seems that'll have to do, but it makes me feel, somehow, cheated; dissatisfied. And I don't have any record of when I was there. Not one picture of the baby with me there, too.

My possible subjects are certainly limited now. I imagine that people like me would tend to have fewer close relatives and most of our friends would tend to be dead. So there's nobody left to take pictures of but strangers and ourselves when the papers tell me that strangers and old ladies shouldn't mix and, at no time, have I ever been a beauty. Not bad in the face, but no tits. I never used to say that word but nobody seems to mind now and neither do I. I lost a lot of weight in my twenties and your tits are always the first things to go. Not even having Susan altered that. In any case, even if I'd got the chance, I wouldn't have wanted pictures of myself.

It's funny, I do have some snapshots from one time I went away, but I would rather I had nothing left at all. If I think of all the films I went to see – Garbo, Deitrich, Virginia Lake, Bogart and Spencer Tracy, even Ronald Coleman – the films they made are just as good now as they were when I saw them new, but those two little pictures a stranger took of Archie and me, look as if we're dead and buried, years ago. We haven't kept well.

Me and Archie should have been a film. A woman at the bowling club told me that her nephew had appeared on television. Four years ago, this was, before I had the fall. He was in a quiz, apparently, with prizes and they brought him down to London with his wife, paid for their room in a lovely hotel and sent them on a guided tour. She said she took a video of the programme, but what's the point? He'll be on for a couple of minutes, be made to look a fool and that'll be it. He didn't win.

By now, they'll all have done it. They're nice enough people, but I know what they're like. They'll all have gone off and done something, just to keep up. The last time I was there it was getting on the radio. That was the thing that everyone had to do. They asked for dedications, or called up and gave their opinions, or answered questions. There were quizzes then, too. You couldn't tell them it was nothing, only noises in the air. Nice enough people, like I say.

I have come to the conclusion that I deserve better things, that's all. I know I'll not get them, but that's fine. I would rather be content in hoping and making my position clear than settle for lies and nonsenses and second best. I will take pictures of the things which are important so that I can keep them to look at again and, one day, I will maybe make a film.

When I couldn't go out to bowl any more and I hadn't thought of photographs, it turned out that I started watching films at the cinema. I am very lucky in where I live; once I've got down the stairs from the second floor, I have only to walk round the corner and the supermarket's right there. I can make the Botanic Gardens on my better days and, behind, me there are grocers and bakers and the whole of the Byres Road, right down to Partick. I also have my pick of two cinemas. The both of them seemed a bit shabby, which is why, I think, I'd never gone before, but one afternoon I was already out and I started feeling tired and then, along with all the other poor souls, I was drifting into the pictures, really for the sake of company.

That time it was Robert De Niro, whom I'd already seen in something with my daughter in Leicester Square. He was very good. Here they changed the features almost every week and the one place had a choice between two films, because they'd cut the screen in half to make two small ones, and, of course, I went back after that. I got very keen.

You'll believe me if I tell you, but you won't understand, that when leaving your home for a pint of milk has to be planned in advance and you know you won't bump into friends while you're out because most of them are dead, it tends to throw you back on yourself. You either get dottled, or you think a lot, or sometimes both.

It seems strange to me now that our painters and our poets and our novelists aren't all of them sixty-five and over. How could you get the time to think and imagine properly when there's people and money and children and things going on? I don't know how they manage it when they're younger. I suppose they must just want to do it very much. I do know I have to do it very much, or end up like Mr McShane at the Tuesday Club, who spends half of his time in Spain in the Civil War and the rest of it talking to chairs and feeling himself. I don't want to die in public in a hospital, or some institutional lounge where I've dragged around for years, forgetting myself and smelling more and more of my own piss. That clingy, awful straw and honey smell of stale piss. The Tuesday Club at the Centre is thick with it. If you say pensioner to me it's the first thing

85

that comes to mind.

There are brighter things to think of, though. For instance, I make a point of remembering past events, because I want to be sure that I always know what's happened and what's now. If you practice that every day, you can tell the difference. I make lists of bills and shopping, to keep myself straight and then, when I've done my exercise, when I've proved all the cogs still fit, I can put a cassette into my player and I can start imagining.

You have to be very careful when you imagine and you're alone. Some people I've seen have locked themselves up in their heads and swallowed the key. They can't get out. Even when it seems you're doing fine, you can slip into wishful thinking so easily. I must have spent months in the Spring and Summer just after my fall, running through what I would do at the bowling club. Several of the ladies and the couples have cars and all of them offered to come and take me down there, as soon as the season began. I wouldn't be able to do much, they realised that, but I could sit at the side and watch them, enjoy the crack. They said it would be company for me. I was silly and looked forward to it all – what I would wear, the rugs and thermoses needed, what a sharp observer I would make. Naturally, nobody came. I haven't seen one of them since.

Now I'm careful with my thinking. Going to the cinema helps; it gives me ideas. Particularly, Robert De Niro gives me ideas.

I look at him, and the other ones like him, and they spend so much time and energy on just looking ordinary. There are lights and backgrounds and special effects and music – that's a very important thing – and all of this is there to make them look better than ordinary. They want to look everyday. When Meryl Streep wakens up in a film, she'll want to look as if she's been to sleep, only, she'll seem much more wonderful, because films look at people so nicely, they can't help seeming wonderful. I have an idea that the ordinary people should be in the films. They wouldn't have to waste their time forgetting they were stars and they would get their chance to be wonderful. This means that I now spend some of my thinking time imagining films for people that I know. Sometimes, for people that I love. The best one is my mother's film. That's the best one of all.

My mother was two different people; one of them is hard to remember, the other one I've only heard about. If I'd been older when I knew her, I could have understood her more, but you always miss the best of your mother with only being a child while she's there. I only knew she was a mixture of things.

When she was alone, or thought she was, you would sometimes hear her singing in her birdy, pipey voice. When I heard it first, I thought it was someone outside, or a stranger with her, and then I got to our door and the music stopped and, when I looked in, there was nobody there but her. She didn't have a face you'd think would sing, there was something wary in it, something closed, but that day in the room, even when she had stopped herself and was hiding her song away, there was still a glow about her. It was slow to fade. That was the first time I wondered what age she was.

I always knew it was her when she sang after that, whether the words were strange ones in Gaelic, or springy ones you'd heard whistled in the street. I would try sometimes to be quiet and still on the stair and wait to listen to her through the door.

The only other times I saw that shine about her came when she told me stories she made up. My father might take the boys out on a Sunday and, if he did, there would just be my mother and me alone and, if it had been a good day, there might be a story for me when I asked. She spoke about a country full of names I couldn't say which had animals and mountains and was never too far from the sea. I think now, she was telling me her childhood and that was why it often made her sad.

Her sisters, when I met them later, told me she always sang when she was young. They described a light, laughing woman, who had danced until her cheeks and forehead flushed and who either cried because she was too happy, or because she had a daft, soft heart. The woman I remembered was older and pale with concealing a sickness that no one else could reach. At meals, she served herself the smallest portion and barely took a peck from out of that. She saved up her tears for the wash house, where they could join sweeter waters and my father wouldn't see.

Mother died when I was eleven and left me with the man who had eaten up her joy. He made me understand her weeping and the noises that had wakened me in the night. I wouldn't

87

make a film for him. All that I want to recall of him is I'm glad of the way he died and couldn't have prayed for better, or been more satisfied. Drunk at his work, he crushed his hips to nothing under a girder. And other people told me, so it must be true, that he squealed and screamed for hours before the end. I think of him in that wee ambulance, leaving the yard and it makes me think less of myself, but I can't be sorry.

For my mother, I've thought of a film where she could be happy. This one could have launched her in her new career and recorded just a little of her joy. I have made it a Gainsborough film, with that lovely, faded kind of colour that would have been more comfortable for her eyes. The story would remind you of Jane Austen, but the dresses would be prettier. Mother would wear dozens of them to sing and play, to dance in brilliant candle light, or to walk across lawns of emerald green and fall gently and deeply in love. Her hair would be long and, when it was freed, it would shine, it would spark in her eyes. People who had never met her, would all agree how beautiful she was and, instead of disappearing when I die, she would be a part of us; a star. That would be no more than she deserves.

My films are only silliness, I know, but I enjoy them and they help me set things right. I want there to be something to say I was here; that all of us were here, and that sometimes we have felt we were discontented. If I could be the first pensioner film director, I would make films about us. I wouldn't choose anyone special, like a spy, or a general, who might be remembered, or famous for anything else. I would film an ordinary person, their story, because they have good stories, too. Someone should remember them. I don't think the public would feel they'd been disappointed. In fact, because of the way that films make you look at things, I don't think they would notice a difference.

Even I have a story. It wouldn't be one that I could use, I'm not so proud of myself as that, but if somebody would film it, it would be good. I would like to leave something behind me to say that the dottled old woman who walks on two sticks and shows slides to the Tuesday Pensioner's Club did have a story. Things happened to her.

The film would have things to explain. I hear the young women in the Centre where they hold our club and I think they live in harder times than we ever did, but if I showed them how it felt to eat and sleep and cook and wash and mark off the years of your children and your living in the one square of a room, maybe they would wonder why there hadn't been a bigger change since then. I know I never had time for such thoughts when I was younger. I wasn't angry that I lost two babies, only glad my little Susan thrived.

My children had a father, of course, to share the room; a good man who worked hard. Tam. He took me away from my father and brothers which only a good man would have done. We had to move north of the river after that and leave our friends behind. I hardly ever saw Tam drunk and he never hit me, he was tender in his way, but I hated him. I hated all the hours spent with the two of us penned up in that room. I hated myself for using him to get away from another room and, at night, although he was gentle, I hated the smell and the touch of him. Now, my father would have got the jail for what he did to me, but what was done would still have been done, and I would still have been the way I was. Tam believed that I was shy.

We did the thing that films always want you to do; we moved into a wee bit better place and, slowly, we could feel more safe. Tam was a painter to trade and, although the quality customers went elsewhere, he built a business for himself. By the time the other painter was in Poland with his troops, Tam had three men on his books.

I met Archie when the war was two years over and Tam was busy setting up again. Archie wasn't fair. The first time we were properly alone together, it was a winter afternoon. Dusk was falling and he took my hand in the street and made me stop. He looked up.

That's the first star, Margaret, you should make a wish.

He knew that wasn't fair. He knew what I would wish.

The film would show how easy it is to be unfaithful to a busy man and how easy it is to want something beautiful. It would show me my happiness. We would be singing as Archie drove his car out past Milngavie and his arm would be round my waist as we walked in the grass. A low, dry stane dyke had fallen away on a slope and he stepped across the flat spread of stones. My shoes were a little slippy, unsuitable, and he reached his hand down to pull me up. That would only be a tiny moment in the picture, but it would show our hands and faces and be slow and watch the way that people choose things they'll remember. I could tell you how warm the sun was, that the breeze smelt of the morning's rain and which birds sang. It made me cry – that one movement he'd made without thinking. It told me too much about him, too suddenly. His grip was too sure and gentle. His strength was too reliable. He felt as if he might be a giving man and as if he might care. I had never wanted to meet the right man for me. I had never had the space for hopes like that and then Archie made me feel he had finally come when everything was all too late.

I told Tam I was poorly and I needed some time to myself. He didn't mind; he would take care of Susan. He imagined I was going to a friend in the country. I took a taxi to the railway station and Archie met me there with his car. We stayed in a little hotel away in Argyll and for four days I was Mrs Sturrock and not Mrs Mackintosh.

I wouldn't want to show our love . I never saw it, because my eyes were closed. I heard my voice in a strange, close bedroom, telling him about my father; I told Archie everything. I woke up each of the mornings, wanting to look at him. I wanted him to be still sleeping so that I could watch his face and wake him when I snuggled up because I liked touching him. The last morning I cried. We told the young man at reception that I was feeling unwell when we came down with our cases and I was so pale. We said it would be better if we just started off for home. He smiled.

Tam never believed a word of it, when I told him. He was a very settled, confident man, so he couldn't believe it. It almost made him laugh. I seemed to disappear when he was like that. I was so used to him being right, it was very difficult to be sure that he was wrong. I had to keep the picture of Archie very clear in my head. In the end, there was nothing left but for Tam to be angry. Susan was in from school; she was nearly seven, then, and his shouting brought her in from her room. She looked white and worried and we shouldn't have sent her away again so upset, but we did. And when she had closed the door, Tam told me that, in any case, of course I would never leave because, if I did, I wouldn't see Susan again.

The next day I wrote to Archie in a letter I didn't send. I told him that I loved him, which I hadn't said before, and then I tore it up. I tore it up and didn't send another and, when I was meant to meet him next, I didn't go. I hope he understood, but I think that it's far more likely that I hurt him and he hated me, which is a shame because I did love him. He never tried to get in touch.

So, I stayed with Tam and Susan and life was sometimes uncertain and sometimes comfortable. My daughter got into a nice school and learned to be different from us. I waited and, when I was fifty-three, Tam died. Susan came back from London for the funeral. It was good to have her stay here for a while.

I think I would finish my film with the funeral, because there isn't much that happened after that. What there is seems very personal, anyway, as it happened when my time was all my own. I don't know if I'd want it seen in public. Increasingly, there seem to be only tiny patches in my life that are at all important. There are images, or moments. It's material more suited to a series of photographs.

Bix

He knew he was about to think of Maggie. She was in the air and on the way like thunder. This time it was the sound of her kiss. A sound of eating, of biting ripe fruit, of drinking and licking him up as if he was something nourishing and hot. It was always unmistakable and so loud. You would suppose that, in the quiet of the night, a kiss might well be noticed, especially close by the ear, but their nights had never been quiet. The railway battered past their window on a cutting above the back court with trains running into the small hours and then dragging by for repairs. There were cars and cat fights and anxious dogs, the drunk man down the stair and air in the pipes and above it all, their breathing as they roamed about the bed. Still Maggie's kisses would echo and shout, driving all the rest of it away.

The time would arrive when they lay without sleeping, side against side, and he would touch her to feel the last of her sweat. Between the curve of her stomach and the bone of her hip he would circle with his fingertips, find the place, then brush and twirl across it: the other side, too. That gave her little shivers which she liked. Sometimes these would lower her into sleep and sometimes they would make her start again. You never knew which until it happened.

The rain was harder now, twisting down in the wind and

92

lifting back off the pavements in a haze. His hair had been needing washed, but now it would just look wet. Better to have an umbrella, though, or a hat. He would walk over west a little and find a bar. He was going to have a drink.

His drinking hadn't made Maggie leave him. He was sober when she went away. They didn't know each other when he started and it didn't seem she'd noticed when he stopped. For a time, when he was newly dry, he made a point of taking Maggie to the pictures. He made sure to arrive in time to watch the adverts, to sit beside his wife as the screen was filled with ice and lemon and slender girls in bikinis, plunging through rum. All they ever seemed to advertise was salted nuts and booze and he sat and stared them out, unblinking. He wanted her to see that he was strong. Then, one evening, after something funny, not the kind of film that she enjoyed, Maggie turned to him as they left and reached the street.

'Well, I'm away to Preston's for a while. I haven't seen that crowd for ages, with you and your moods. Don't worry, I'll not be late. Not all of us can't handle it, you know.'

That was the end of the pictures. Him and his moods.

But she had loved him, she had loved him very well. She wanted to be pretty for him; she told him that, time and again. He could alter the length of her dresses, the shade of her lips, with a couple of words. Such power. She had cut her hair as he suggested and kept her legs and underarms shaved smooth, even asked if he would like her shaved elsewhere. She would have done it, too. Probably waited to surprise him, calling him in to watch her lather up. Enough of that.

It was only very slowly that she changed, the process beginning with her mouth. One by one, all her vowel sounds seemed to stretch. She managed to make the word gas rhyme with arse. She was very careful not to say youse, but only you. Sometimes, she sounded so strangled and uncomfortable, that he had to laugh. That made her angry and so he told her she was fooling no one and that made her angrier still.

He thought for a while she had a lover and was taking these pains for him, as her dresses and perfumes were gradually transformed. Then he realised. Every time she left the house Maggie was outshining him. Contrary to popular belief, he had been the first to show his age: just a touch of weight that he lost again, the hair not thin, but certainly turning grey and, of course, he'd still been drinking then, so he was getting slow. On the other hand, she still looked good; they both knew it. Standing next to him, she looked even better. She had seen it all happening and made up her mind. She encouraged the little smiles, the admiring comments, but now she added to them, now she could have her public's sympathy. Poor woman; intelligent, attractive and stuck with a sagging drunk.

That wasn't fair. She'd known she was getting on a wee bit and splashed out, that was all. It was his fault if he hadn't measured up. Blaming your failures on other people was a thing his friends had told him not to do. These were the friends that had kept him on the wagon by getting him to understand himself. They had also told him not to look for reasons because knowing why you did a thing wasn't the way to stop; it was only a way of putting decisions off. Still, he'd thought enough about it by then to know that whatever the reason was, it wasn't his wife. He owed his friends a lot, perhaps his life. It was a shame he hadn't seen them for a while.

He marched through the fading shower and wished for one of those blue, unsteady days. They had walked out together often, Maggie and himself, enjoying such days. It had been Summer – it was now – but it was a brighter Summer then. On Sundays they would head along the broad road out of town with a whipping, directionless wind taking the heat out of the sun. It would push at their coats and twirl their hair and rush the clouds above them, so the light fell like someone playing with a switch.

Days like that you could feel the river. You knew it was there all the time, behind the houses, but then you could feel it, you could smell it turning into sea. Everything was moving West; you, the clouds and Maggie and the river. You could feel the river, how alive it might be, slipping in between the grey spaces where the dead yards used to be, the new, red brick apartments and the empty docks.

The only place near them that you could see the river was where they'd cleared an old yard away and left them with open ground and the stubble of walls. There the river didn't look much, just a wee, grey rectangle with sometimes flecks of sun to prove it was moving.

The woman beside him, for all those Sundays, was Maggie. He must have been awful to be with for her to grow so changed. At the time, he hadn't thought so, but that must have been the way of it.

He chose this bar because he was tired and his eyes had started to ache. When he pressed his fingers against them, only lightly against the lids, it hurt so much that it scared him and he stopped. The music here was American; big band stuff, Swing and Glen Miller, too late for his tastes. Not like his 78s: his wee collection with all his raw and bawdy, melancholy friends. He wished they would play Ella, Louis, Velma Middleton, but most of all, Frankie Trumbauer, or just anyone playing with Bix. Sweet Bix Beiderbecke. He sat down and stared at the table until he was sure he wouldn't cry.

The waitress was dressed like all the others. Green and white candy striped blouse, little green waistcoat, white apron, black trousers and a green bow tie. It made her look fat. She didn't smile, perhaps because he didn't. He picked a hot chocolate from the menu and looked across at the bar as she moved away. It was very clean, with mahogany stained wood and brass and mirrors, no ash trays, or beer mats and here he was, sitting in an armchair with his elbows on a marble table top and behind him, a white plaster statue of a woman, clutching a sheet in a way that covered neither of her tits. She looked uncomfortable and Greek. They had a nice wind-up gramophone, a Columbia, some pseudo Thirties junk and several clocks, but they also looked uncomfortable and they made the rest of the place seem too new. It was all like their music: digital Glenn Miller and schmaltz. They wouldn't know real style from a kick in the head. And he was angry for being expected to feel out of place. Next time round he'd have a half and a whisky and then they'd see. People like them had been safe since he'd got sober.

Maggie would have liked it here, in fact, she probably did. It wasn't too far from her office. She must have come in. She would arrive with the girls, the ones that she needed to please, four or five of them, all laughing, in broad shouldered jackets and tight, little matching skirts. If they went after work, then Maggie would take a wee drink. A double Grouse, straight, no ice. Then she would take another and then she would start.

Indeed? I wouldn't have thought so.

That was what she always said and the people who were with her; strangers, acquaintances, friends; they wouldn't know what to expect. They wouldn't know that, if Maggie hadn't thought it, then the thing could not be so. But she never argued, that was a thing she didn't do. Maggie gave you the facts as she saw them and if you didn't agree, she would give you them again, only this time, more slowly, so that you would understand. She was right and you were daft and that was it.

People laughed, or were offended and, whichever way, they left. Maggie didn't know this hurt him; that he had once punched a man in a toilet because he had laughed at her and said it was a sin she was out without her mother. He would come back to their table with his round and he would feel ashamed. She made herself so ugly and stupid and loud. Back home he would be angry because she had made him ashamed of his own wife and left him to brood on the guilt of that. It hadn't hurt his pride, that wasn't affected, he'd been surprised when someone had suggested that. He only hated being made ashamed.

The hot chocolate came in a white china mug with the name of the place around it in green letters. He wondered what kind of people came here. Who would arrange to meet in a place like this, with a name he would be embarrassed to say out loud ? The waitress took his money, there and then, as if she didn't trust him not to leave without paying.

He decided he would leave without drinking. They would clear away the mug, still full, and cold, with a skin across it from the milk and that would let them know how much he thought of them. He would go away. This wasn't the place.

The evening he made her go he wanted to kiss her. He wanted to put his lips on her lips and lick between her teeth with his tongue. To feel the way she was snug and hard against him, comfortable and living and new, and to be surprised in the way he was always surprised when she tasted so much like him, he wanted that. He would have lifted her skirt and pulled her tight in and told her she was beautiful, but he couldn't do that. Not one part of that, could he do.

'Maggie. Maggie ? Listen. Could you? Please?'

They had been watching television, a documentary about

turtles and their eggs. He had sat a few feet away from her, knowing she was there and he must tell her, while the thousands of soft, baby turtles emerged from their sandy nests and began to die. Those who had escaped the egg thieves were mainly eaten or shrivelled up, as they pattered their way to the sea where most of the remainder would be killed. It made him depressed. He chose to tell her then. More than anything, to stop himself thinking of turtles all night.

'Maggie?'

'What is it?'

'I was talking to you.'

'I know. Can't it wait ten minutes for the end ? Anyway, you know where the kettle is.'

This was the woman he had married because he had wanted to. She had carried her joy and love for him like a baby. The nursing of it had made her a second Mary, beautiful and serene and making the flesh and blood children they couldn't have, superfluous. Or so it seemed. She had been his glory.

'I don't want a cup of tea. I want to talk.'

'Not now. It's nearly time for bed. Tomorrow evening. I'm tired now, alright? You always pick your moment, don't you?'

'I know that, I'm sorry.'

'Oh, for Christ's sake. I'll go and put the kettle on. Just don't you bloody shift yourself, will you.'

And so the news he had caught her, as she opened the sitting room door.

'Barbara that I work beside, you don't know her. For two years, we've been screwing. I'm sorry. You'll want a divorce.'

Maggie never spoke. She just stood there and he didn't try to look at her face, so he couldn't remember now how it had been. A handful of turtles finally swayed out to sea and he heard her breathing, as if she was winded, and then she left.

At one point, he heard her call a taxi and, when it blew his horn, she came down the stair with two cases. He was waiting.

'You'll be away to your mother's. I understand. Tell her that I'm sorry, because I am.'

She put down her cases and punched the side of his head, in what seemed one continuous movement. Then her knee came up sharp against his balls, none too squarely, but enough, and she was gone.

That night, or to be more exact, the following morning, when the luminous blue of a clear dawn was rising into his house, he tried to phone her. He had sweated out the night in a haunted bed. The hollow weight of her absence beside him kept him awake more completely than her presence ever had. The smell of her had lain all around him and so he had changed the sheets, pulled off the pillow slips, found a fresh coverlet, but she was still there. As soon as he started to doze, she would brush against him and he would feel the small disturbance of her breath.

By the telephone in the hall it was cooler. His mouth was bitter and sticky and a sick, dragging tiredness made the room swing whenever he turned his head, but he would call her and she would answer, because she was his wife would know it was him calling because of what time it was. Probably she couldn't sleep herself.

But he couldn't dial the number. Then, when he did dial, he imagined he'd got it wrong and cut himself off before he was half way through. He dialled again and the number was right and again he couldn't let the call connect. He stopped dialling. A pulse had started up in his stomach and his hands began to shake. He let himself slide down the wall, let it chill his back, and he sat on the floor with the telephone held in his hands. His first day without her was coming and was cold and he didn't know how he could call her and he didn't know what he could say. He found that he was crying and it hurt.

He got through later, he didn't know how much later, and the line was engaged. Every time, engaged. It made him feel stupid and alone.

There was no more rain, the cloud was breaking up and it was colder. It would be a cold night. He cut between the flowers, across the square, and spat. The sound was good, definite, and he wanted to be rid of something, if only that. Also, Maggie had hated him to spit. Across the road, there was the station, all lit up.

Many married men love other women and have neat affairs. Many men lie to their wives with great success. Their secrets are slowly forgotten and their marriages remain intact. How many men tell their wives they have loved elsewhere when this is a

98

hurtful lie and will make them leave ? But he had done that. He had made all of her leave: her soft, hot feet, her perms and highlights, the taste of stale whisky, waiting in her gentrified mouth. One evening, back from Preston's, she had kissed him like that. He remembered her slack, wet lips and her little, fat tongue; stubby and tangy with scotch.

Lips that touch liquor shall never touch mine.

And he pushed her away. She had woken him that night with an elbow in his ribs which had left a bruise. Gradually, he became aware of her, lying on her back, rocking and jerking and letting out moans. He had turned to her and kissed her shoulder, caught her hands.

'What are you doing?'

'What do you think? It's a better time than I ever get with you. Go back to sleep and leave me alone.'

A little while later he heard her come, then felt her settle down to sleep. He thought he should shake her awake again and fuck her; she'd still be wet. Then it came, still and clear in his mind, that he would sleep now, too, and be rid of her entirely, later on. In the process, if he could hurt her, he would be pleased.

There was no one that he worked beside called Barbara. In his life he had slept with three other women, all of them before Maggie, and once he was engaged, he had, as they said in the songs, been constant and true. He was not, he thought, faithful by nature, but his love for Maggie, really, love, and then later his isolation from suitable female friends, had meant he remained constant and true. From the times when this would set her weeping in his arms, they moved to her snide, over confident days, when she told him, among other people, that his bottle was all away to Hell. And there were other things she said he no longer had: it was odd that she should knee him in them, when she'd always been so certain they were gone. Just making sure, no doubt.

He stepped into the station, smiling. The place was mostly deserted; one sleeping train, a few people walking with coffee in paper cups, or just waiting for others to come, or themselves to go. He knew there was a bar here. It took its name from a well-known Scottish river, now flanked by decaying industries and sites for exclusive housing developments. The river he was born by. He went in.

A middle aged woman in white stilettos picked her way to the toilets at the back of the room. Her heels were unevenly worn, so she tottered and sometimes slid. Lieutenant Columbo watched her from the television set above the fruit machine.

She was almost the only woman, apart from the one behind the bar, and he felt at home. It was right being here. It was like what he'd seen in a film once where the restaurant at an airport had tables for the passengers in transit sectioned off. They had left but they hadn't arrived yet, so they were nowhere and they were kept away from the others in case the nowhere spread. He remembered that.

This was a nowhere; a less expensive one. You could drink here until you couldn't drink any more and stand here until you couldn't stand any more and you needn't be sad or angry when nobody cared. There was nobody here to. Nobody to be guilty, or ashamed. No body. No where.

Shite. He should just order and make a start.

Then he was afraid. He shouldn't do this. He couldn't trust himself to do this, because he knew that he couldn't be trusted, that this had been shown. The brandy glass with the china cat peering over the lip had shown it. In the morning it had been smashed and in the fireplace; the china cat, a headless, tailless cat; as if it had been hit by a china car. He didn't find a replacement for that, although with many other things, he did. The bruise around Maggie's eye with the tiny cut had sorted itself. He could only cry when he woke and saw that, not remembering how it had happened, but knowing it must have been him. Sometimes he lost his grip on things a little, that was a fault.

But all of that had stopped. The breaking and the drinking had stopped and he had bought her new things. Then she set in with her dusting and methodically, maliciously, broke them all. He had replaced almost everything and bought her other presents besides and she had broken them all. In the end, he believed there was nothing left to break; hearts being soft, pulsing organs, only broken in songs. Then Maggie had come back and broken his songs.

There was no way of telling when. It could have been only

100

a day after she left him, it could have been when she came back to fetch her things, it could have been any time when he was out, because she kept her key. Whenever and however, by degrees or all in one rush, Maggie had gone to his cupboard and done this thing, intentionally, to hurt him. She had taken out each of his 78s, felt the fat, black weight of them, seen the ripple in the fine grooved surface, like satin or watered silk, and she had broken every one. Not smashed, broken into large, irregular pieces all of which had been fitted together again and replaced in their brittle, paper sleeves.

Bix Beiderbeck was broken. All of him. Bix, the inspirational, the biting, unrepeatable, lyrical Bix. Bix, whose parents had sat at home, his letters to them unopened, thinking of piano lessons wasted. Bix who was fond of a wee refreshment, who liked his drink. Bix who died young and made things alright because drunks who died young were romantic; they'd paid for the damage they'd done. It wasn't as good if you managed to stay alive.

When he found what had happened he hadn't known what to do. He went through them all when he discovered. Columbia, HMV, Brunswick, Parlophone; sleeves advertising needles and gramophone repairs, he searched through them slowly, then fast, then very slowly, as he knew he was coming to the end. All gone. Maggie was a very thorough woman. He had truly hated her then. Things had not been right with him ever since.

Bix was gone.

The poor souls

Last night, I had a thought. Snow is like bad news. When you walk on your own and it falls at the first, out of that thick, silent sky, it is almost frightening. Unnatural. Rain can be brisk, or playful, fat, bitter, salt, but always it will fall in a natural way. It will fall like a waterfall; like pouring sand, perhaps deflected by breezes, because it is a light thing, but you can always understand it. The speed it has gathered running through the air, the noises it makes when it lands, rain you can understand. The smothering, covering snow, creeping down the sky and pulling the eye down with it is different. It hypnotises, down and down and down, changing everything without a sound. Like bad news.

I only mention this because once I met a woman on a train who was terrified of snow and now I can understand a little of why that was. But I can't be sure what other people think, or of what she thought. Perhaps she was only scared of freezing to death.

The trains are good when there's snow. It tears beside the windows in white threads and you look out from the warm on melting streets and pale, blank allotments with dog tracks. The canal disappears.

I travel by train a great deal because I no longer have to pay.

This isn't a formal arrangement. The appropriate authorities have never been informed. But all of them know. I don't pay.

If an inspector catches sight of me in a carriage he will pass it by, or if he enters, he ignores me politely and I return the compliment by affecting the general air of a passenger who has paid. If I am seen at a station, word will be sent down the track and often the whole of my journey will be passed without inspection.

The people who live by the line, I have noticed, forget that we are there. They assume we don't look up at their windows, or that we travel too fast to see. At night they embrace, cook supper and undress but, most of all, they stand in front of the glass with their curtains open and look at their own reflections laid over the dark. They must think, they must imagine, and we rattle through their hopes and memories, without ever feeling a thing.

The hospital was very near the station. We were sometimes allowed to go down to take a trip. The women were sent east for shopping and the men were sent out west to fish in the sea. I still see them on the platform, the poor souls, the ones they will keep. Their hair has been cut efficiently and they wear clothing they didn't choose, each item marked with a label and their name in indelible ink.

Pat will sometimes be there. She runs from the trains with her carrier bags heavy and full, the cigarette nailed in her mouth. Short, hungry puffs. Her face is closed. It tells you she is chasing something which she cannot let be, it doesn't say what. And Pat has never said anything at all.

Different young women follow her.

Pat, can I carry your bags? Pat? Pat, can I carry your bags?

Terry and I had no interest in fish, or shops, so we took our outings together, convalescing by train. We went to the Green on bright weeks, rode and looked from the carriage when it rained.

I miss Terry. There are sections of the line I still can't travel without feeling sad.

He went out a few days before me and I didn't see him again. I heard they had him back for a while, just a wee while. They let him go again the same week and he stood in a basin of water in his kitchen at home and blew himself clean through the window with a cable plugged into the mains. It was in the paper. That's how I know.

I don't use the station by the hospital, not any more. I just pass through.

Terry was better than the average. Terry gave everyone a chance. You had the feeling he was just there as a favour, because he knew that other people were and he thought they might appreciate a chat. He was the only person Ken would let shave him, all the nurses couldn't stop talking about that. I suppose he must really have joined us because he had troubles in his head. He can't have got them sorted out. Or maybe they were sorted out too well. The second time I met him I told him I'd killed my husband and I thought he ought to know. If he didn't want to speak to me again, I wouldn't mind. I would have minded but I wanted to be honest with him rather than have him find out.

You killed your husband?

Yes.

Doesn't worry me. I don't intend to marry you. No offence. Do you mind if I ask, have you ever killed anyone else?

Of course not. No.

But you did kill him.

Yes.

It wasn't an accident.

No. Well, I've often thought, if I was married, I would want to kill my wife. That's why I live on my own, by the way.

So that's him. I remember what he looked like. I know that he lived alone. I read there was nobody with him when he died. And whenever they gave him rice pudding he kicked up a fuss. He said it was only fit for folk with no teeth. That isn't much to leave behind you. He should have had more than that; more than just a place in my head.

There are dead times on the trains, especially at night. There's no one left, looking forward to the city and it's too soon for anyone else to be coming back home. A station will appear under its lights, pull up close and float to a stop, then the doors to every carriage will slide apart. They're automatic. Even if the platform was deserted they would open, just the same. It can make me afraid. I can be sitting there, all by myself, perhaps only two or three of us for the whole length of the train, and we stop and the doors slip open and nothing steps in but the chill above the track.

You wonder. I wonder. What if they let in passengers I can't see? What if older travellers come back?

That doesn't make any sense. The night thoughts that touch you never make any sense. But the seats around me can sometimes begin to feel occupied. They begin to watch. I imagine that Terry might be there. My husband, too.

Terry's face is like a photograph in my head; all the detail is there, while my husband is very faint. Almost invisible. He is still too familiar to be clear and I never did have a picture of him, so there's nothing I could check. It's a shame. I know he had such lovely eyes.

We met in the Botanic Gardens. In the Palace, with the ferns. You come in past a statue in waxy, white stone of a naked man with a monkey perched on his thigh. The glass-house was almost empty; an old Sikh on one of the benches in Temperate Asia; wet moss and weeping banana leaves. I was looking at something small with red flowers when a man with beautiful eyes came up and talked to me. He bought us both an ice cream from the van parked at the gate and we ate them, then walked through the park all afternoon. We took it slowly and sometimes sat. There were squirrels like little, grey cats that followed and froze and followed and stood to beg. Before our walk had finished, the man and I had kissed. That time, or the next time. The kisses came early. It was spring.

He loved me to cook for him. Between us we bought the right things: the copper saucepans with wooden handles and the sharp, French knives. We chose each other shining vegetables and strange fruit. I searched for recipes to please him and I cooked. It almost made me glad he could only be home for some of the time. All that cooking I had to do.

Our evenings began when the meal was done. We had sweet, Italian biscuits and oily coffee in the Continental style and, by then, the peat would be reddening in the fire and we could look at it. I would have liked to turn the lights out and watch it properly, but my husband never wanted to. It didn't matter. I could always wait and do that on my own.

My husband only turned the lights out when he wanted to go to sleep. I would have undressed in the bathroom and run into bed in the dark. In the dark, he wouldn't have noticed I closed my eyes. I told him that I listened to poetry and music like that. I told him that I wanted to hear us, to feel and taste and smell us and that looking was for other times and other people. He said if he saw my eyes, he could tell if I was with him or not.

Who else would I be with?

He didn't know.

No, who else, come on?

Nobody else. He was sorry. Maybe he should close his eyes, too.

I still undress for him; by a chair, a little way from the bed. Everything is slower than it should be, more deliberate, as if he was still curled and watching, his shoulders above the covers. Pink.

I dressed for him. Knickers that he would like. Even under trousers, knickers he would find and like. Bras, too. Sweaters that were good to touch, blouses that hung well, there for someone else to appreciate. Now, I don't buy things. I haven't got the money any more, but whatever I wear, it still belongs to him. I suppose that will change in the end.

As soon as I had pushed him, I wanted to pull him back. I definitely tried to catch his hand, but he was reaching for the banister and finding nothing to grip and finally rolling and falling and twisting as he fell. I lived on the second floor, but when I looked over and down, he was lying at the head of the close. His arms were crossed.

The stained glass light in my landing window had just begun to tint the floor. It must have been five in the morning, maybe six, so the colours were blurred soft. I stepped across them and went inside. My husband must have fallen very lightly because nobody seemed to be disturbed. Up and down the stairwell, there wasn't a sound.

He had been leaving to go back to her, in the way that he always did. No matter how long he stayed; a night, a weekend, a week; it was never completely out of mind. That time when his shirts and knickers and cigarettes went back into his bag and were taken home to her. To be washed. To have me cleaned away.

It didn't worry me. I knew he had never loved her. It didn't worry me a bit.

Then I thought, before I closed the door behind him, that this was as far as we would ever go. He wasn't going to marry me. He wasn't going to make himself my husband properly, although I could no longer be anything but his wife. I had kissed him goodbye and tightened the scarf at his throat and seen for the very first time there was no hope. We were wasting each other. We had been wasting away, all this time. We were hardly there. I wished he would go quickly because he didn't like it when I cried and then I ran out from the doorway and gave him that push. But I definitely tried to catch his hand.

At the hospital, later, I learned about snow and bad news. That was what they taught you there. The bitterwhite snow was everywhere: in rooms and in halls, down corridors, they kept it all fresh with snow. Terry and I wrote notices and cut out pictures for the walls. By morning each was buried, drifted away.

They told me I wasn't a widow. I had never had a husband. I couldn't wear black. Nobody had died at the foot of my stairs.

Ridiculous. If I hadn't killed him, he would have come to visit me while I was there. I was his wife. Because of this and other things, for a long time I wanted to leave. Only Terry made it better than it was.

We're living through enlightened days now, hen. Time was, they'd have hung you. Think on that.

Terry kept me sane. He told me people's troubles could be catching and taught me how to touch them and still stay well. It was something about a lightness in your hands. I often wish he was here, taking care of me. After he died that way I didn't think I'd see him again. Now I am sure that I will. I don't need to wish any more, just to wait. Terry will be like my husband. He will want to make me happy and take care of me and he will come back.

This is the most remarkable thing. I don't believe in Heaven, or in God, or really in ghosts, but I do believe in what I saw. My husband knew that I missed him and how sorry I was for what I'd done and so he decided to comfort me with a sign. I do believe in signs.

He waited until I was living at home again. In the hospital too many people were there to notice him, to touch him with their troubles. And I think he was jealous of Terry, although I never gave him cause to be. He waited until I was walking away the evening one time in Spring and put it into my head to go past the gardens where we met. The lights were pushing the domes of the glasshouse up into the dark and casting green shadows from under hot, wet fronds. It was very nice. The gates were locked for the night and I walked on, thinking of him. Across the road there were bars and restaurants, late night shops, all of them bright. And he was there.

He was sitting in the window of the pizza house, at a table with a woman and a laughing boy. They ate and talked together. It was plain they loved each other: father, mother, only son.

I watched them very closely from across the street. The mother and child were sketchy. To be honest they were blurred, but my husband was perfectly in focus. He was very real. He turned and his face looked through me and then he turned away and I knew. He had wanted to show me what we could have become; to tell me I should still have had hope. If I had just kept faith with him, we could have been that family now. I shouldn't have been so frightened because he would have made everything alright. I could almost hear his voice behind me; chiding, but tender; smiling and close.

Cap O'Rushes

It was Christmas and they all had flu. Her husband, her children, herself; they all had flu. It first affected their heads and then it gripped across their chests and, finally, it settled on their stomachs. It made them sick.

She rolled from her side to her back and out of the shape of warmth her lying had left. The new stretch of sheet was just cool enough to be nice.

She thought.

Why had they done it this year? Why had they bothered?

For the children.

But the boys had known what their presents would be in November. There was no surprise. They didn't even like Christmas things: not turkey, or stuffing, or sprouts. No one had felt like eating in any case. The television was awful, they'd seen all the films before on video and they missed their friends from school as soon as the holiday came. Too sick to get away from each other and too well not to care, they sniped and yapped across their room, spilled Ribena in their beds and coughed until they gagged and threw up.

'He was eating my hair gel.'

'No I was not. You'd have to be stupid to eat hair gel.'

'So you are stupid.'

'Not as stupid as you are for wearing it. Poof.'
'Bastard.'
'Fanny.'
'Poof yourself.'

When she was young, her mother read her stories and she'd liked them. Not because she was a little girl, but because she was a little human being. Then she'd read the stories to herself and that was even better. One Sunday morning, she'd woken up, before the birds or the sun, and run to stand and yell in her parents' bedroom.

'I can read! I can read!'
She hadn't realised before.

But now there were centuries and libraries and whole generations of books that belonged to her. Because she could read. She knew their secrets. No one had been as pleased as she was on that Sunday: her mother and father had known she could read for months and had looked at her very strangely, once they were fully awake. Her mother had shouted, but inside, she had probably been pleased. About the reading.

Neither of the boys liked books. They preferred Graphic Novels with pretentious subtexts and violence and sex. She often asked them why they only read comics. When she said this, they would smirk and roll their eyes.

Occasionally, thinking of the books she'd read when she was a little girl, she would look at her sons and see how alien they were. Little boys, little human beings, they liked books. But she had two little changelings. Two little goblin sons.

Then again, she'd married a goblin, so what else could she expect?

In the privacy of her head, her family were The Goblins. That was their name. She couldn't remember deciding, but there it was. No other name could suit them so well. And, because of the terrible flu, the Goblin King and his Goblin Children had gone to their Goblin Grandmother in the West. Such nasty flu. They wouldn't be back for five whole days. Five was her lucky number.

It was fully half past ten before she got up. She had a bath. From the warm of the sheets, to the hot of the bath, to the shiveriness of the underwear and blouse. Having added a skirt and sweater, she made brunch. She felt hungry and better, relaxed.

While she washed up - which somehow she didn't mind doing, just for herself - she ran over her Goblin Lore. She thought of The Signs.

HOW TO TELL YOUR HUSBAND IS A GOBLIN.

She smiled. Colin was a goblin because it was obvious he was a goblin and once you knew he was a goblin, you couldn't think otherwise. There weren't really signs. Nothing infallible. She could have asked her mother what she thought but the answer to the question, 'Is Colin the famous Goblin King of myth and legend?' would have been the same as the answer to 'Will he turn out to be a pervert once I've married him?' or 'Will I regret this decision for the rest of my life?' or 'Is this man an ex-Nazi war criminal, clinging to a double existence as an axe murderer and merchant of child pornography?'

'Yes.'

'Yes.'

'Yes.'

'Yes. Isn't it obvious?'

Mothers never liked their prospective sons-in-law. Not true. Her mother never liked Colin. That was true.

If there was anything which had convinced her that Colin was the Goblin King, then it was probably his shirts. She might as well settle for that.

His shirts, even very new shirts, not yet washed, would change when he put them on. The layers that made up his collars would bubble and peel away from each other, like paint on an old door. His cuffs would ravel and fray while the cloth beneath his armpits yellowed permanently. Clothing seemed to decompose around him and within hours it would seem he had brought it from his grave.

There was something about him rotten. Rotting.

She could imagine his mother receiving him each night from school: scolding and mending and scrubbing away, fighting to send him out in the morning looking as though he was cared for. Had she ever considered there might be something wrong?

111

With him, instead of her? Or had she been a goblin, too.

You couldn't tell now, because she was dead.

She noticed, with the house only free of goblins for one night, it already smelled entirely different. It wasn't that you noticed much while they were there, but there was definitely something missing, now they were gone. There was something they had taken away. In the corners of the rooms, she could still disturb it, as she gathered in their dust: the smell of earth and gravel, damp places and decay. As soon as Colin left, she'd changed their bed and when she woke this morning, she could breathe easily and she felt clean. She usually had a thick head in the mornings.

Her five days passed more slowly than she'd thought. There was time for personal shopping with a lunch in town and she went to the pictures twice; looking at the mothers and fathers with their human, little daughters and sons. She bought books - a great many - more than she'd bought in years and she started to read them carefully, rolling the words round her head to see how they tasted. Night and morning she had a bath, used talcum and perfume, and every day the house grew cleaner and more fragrant along with her. She planted new window boxes and wished it was Spring outside.

The sun set on the fifth day and the rain misted down and she found herself listening for cars in the street below. Almost without thinking, she hid her books away and set four dishes warming, ready for the stew. The goblins were always hungry and always arrived when a meal was on the way. They had very good noses for soups and gravies, in the same way that sharks were sensitive to blood.

The goblin feet stumped on the stair, two pairs of light stumps and one pair that were heavy, and the door was opened with the Goblin King's key. She felt her stomach tighten and knew that if she wasn't careful, her hands would shake.

Years ago, when she had first met Colin, the symptoms had been the same. Waiting in cafés, or on corners, watching for his head to waver above the crowd, she had been equally tense. She had never been sure, when he took her hand, if she smiled because she loved him, or because she knew he wouldn't see her tremble, now that he had her gripped. She didn't know why she was nervous now, except that it was something he shouldn't find out.

It wasn't unusual that she picked at her food. Visitors who saw the goblins eating often had no appetite at all. Colin's jaws would slap together and suck apart, answered by miniature slaps and sucks from his sons. They didn't eat; they consumed. Forks, hands, spoons, were filled, scraps pursued, juices sopped. The mouths were always open, anxious, grim.

She thought she remembered mentioning this to Colin. She thought she remembered him laughing. She thought she remembered him talking about the manly approach to food. This was how men ate. He was bringing his sons up to eat like men. She didn't want them to enjoy their food?

How could she stop them enjoying their food? Goblins always did.

After dinner, the goblins grew drowsy. The blood rushed to their stomachs from their brains and they liked to sprawl in the sitting room for television and sleep. Colin would stay quite quiet until bedtime, but his sons would normally settle for an hour or so and then begin to fret and squirm. Tonight the journey had tired them and they were peaceful.

She washed up and came through to join them, noticing, when she opened the door, that the room now smelt like a cave as she walked in. A cave where someone had recently spilt gravy.

The curtains were tight drawn and only the dead blue glow from the television lit the room. She sat in the armchair facing Colin, watching him. He looked heavy. Stony, in fact. Composed of stones. The hands were broad, flattened by their weight across his knees. They were asleep. His head was only dozing yet, set deep between his shoulders, keeping steady for his eyes and letting them flicker about, or stare, or close.

His eyes were almost closed now, so she could examine him safely. She wondered how he might look on television. How would they present him? Sitting amongst rocks, or feeding, scooping water from a stream? Perhaps mating: they always showed you that. Would other people see him and find him likeable, or would they be aware of that certain strangeness? She thought they would notice the strangeness. Goblins looked very like people, but somehow that made their differences all the more clear. They were disturbing.

Because five was her lucky number she stayed with the goblins another five weeks.

Then, on a Sunday evening, driving through the last of the countryside before the city's light turned into streets, Colin inclined his head a little and asked,

'Well now boys, let's see. How much do you love me today, then, eh? How much? James first.'

'Aw, but Jimmy's always first.'

'That's right. How much do you love me, Jimmy? How much do you love your rotten old dad?'

'Loads. Loads and loads. Honest. I love you more than he does.'

'No you don't.'

'So how much do you love me, William?'

'I love you mountains full. I love you more than anyone else in the whole world.'

'More than anyone at all?'

'Yeah. You're brilliant, Dad. Totally brilliant.'

'Thank you, William.'

'I think you're brilliant, too.'

'I thought he was brilliant.'

'So did I , I just didn't say it.'

'Liar.'

'Fanny.'

'Prick.'

'Boys, boys.'

'He is so a prick.'

'Yes, but you mustn't call him that in front of ladies, William. And your mother is a lady.'

'William got it wrong again.'

'Aye, but at least I'm no a prick.'

She thought that would be the end of it. Usually the end to most of their family discussions was like this. But Colin made the boys be quiet again.

'Boys, be quiet again. As there is a lady present, we should ask her the question, too. What do you think?'

'Aye, go on, Dad.'

114

'Aye, go on.'

'Hmm? So what do you say, wee wifie, how much do you love your old man? How much?'

'Say mountains, mum.'

'Say he's brilliant.'

'Brilliant was my word. Prick.'

She paused to look out of the window. The city was almost upon them now, it wouldn't be long. She saw her face, flat over fields; a string of bungalows; a bridge. She let Colin realise that he was waiting, that she had made him wait, and then she watched her face smile as she told him.

'As much as I can. I love you as much as I can.'

There was no other choice but to go, once that had happened. The Goblin King agreed with her on that.

The office was very nice. When she went there for the interview, she'd liked it. There were posters and lists in marker pen all around the walls and drawings from somebody's child behind one of the desks. On the window ledge there were geraniums: yellow and very leggy, but geraniums all the same.

They'd known that her typing was rusty. She also told them that she'd been married and hadn't worked for several years. The woman asking her questions had looked very serious at that. Then she had explained that all the other applicants for the job had been decidedly inexperienced and that the office was in need of someone a little more dependable.

'You mean older.'

'No. Dependable. But I won't say your age wouldn't be an advantage. People tend not to trust this kind of organisation - if the first person they meet is a twenty-year-old in tie-dyed pyjamas who can't remember where the diary went...'

'I think I know what you mean.'

'She means you'll be our front man. So all of the tie-dyed pyjamas brigade can run amok to themselves in peace.'

The voice came from a man in jeans and a sweatshirt, perched on the corner of a desk beside the window. He held his hand across the mouthpiece of the telephone and smiled, nodding to whatever he was hearing from along the line.

He didn't look like a goblin, but you could never tell.

Colin hadn't known she had a job waiting when she went. He probably hadn't thought it was possible. But it had been. And she had rented a place near the river: two rooms, a kitchen and a bathroom, sectioned out of a large, sandstone house. The newer, thinner walls sounded hollow and frail and the furniture the landlord provided was very tired, but it was fine for now. It smelt of human beings.

When it was finally the last time she would see it, leaving the Goblin's house had been hard. It had been her house, too. And it was warm and comfortable, with nice carpets and ornaments; bits and pieces she had chosen and liked. She arrived in the new place and sat on the rusty sofa, her bags still by the door. She cried a little. Then she unpacked what familiar scents and colours she'd brought with her. She put a sweater to her face, breathing it in, and cried again. But the rooms did change. While she was out at work, something seemed to spread from her books and pictures and, after a month or so, she could come home and not feel a chill of strangeness. Just make a cup of coffee and rest her back.

It was the typing that stiffened her back. She wasn't used to it at all and by lunch time on a busy day, her neck and shoulders would feel almost bruised.

'Just because you're the new girl, you don't have to work too hard. Relax. It's the only way you'll survive in here.'

This time the man was in his shirtsleeves. Still jeans. His smile hadn't changed.

He was far too young, though. Indecently young.

'Don't worry, Ben, I'm alright.'

'Not as green as you're cabbage looking, eh?'

'Something like that.'

'Well, I'll leave you to get on with it.'

'Hmmm.'

She absorbed herself in the pattern of words on her paper until she could feel him drift away.

He was right, of course, she did know what she was doing. She was making herself indispensable. Not that it was very hard. Everyone at the office needed her to be that way.

'Oh, you saved my life. I couldn't think where I'd left it. Thanks again.'

'Could you speak to him. Explain that dancers can't dance on a concrete floor. Their legs break. He'll listen to you.'

'And this is our wonderful secretary. She tells us all where we should be and who we should be with and what we should be doing. Everything. Really. The place couldn't run without her now.'

She smiled when they said these things. She knew they believed they were lying, flattering, but really what they were saying was true. They weren't efficient, so she was. Not too much to be threatening and always very patient, but efficient, too. They wanted to be mothered and organised and to tell their problems to someone they didn't have to know.

They didn't know her. She made sure of that. It was a strength.

In return for their very generous and frequent compliments, she allowed herself to be mystified by their work. She would look at the pots and pictures in their little gallery space, the peculiarly jumbled black and white photographs and she would say nothing. Not even a word. Perhaps she would shake her head, gently, before she went back her files, but that would be all.

Some of the things were actually very nice, but it wouldn't do to tell the artists that. She had to keep them guessing, because that was a strength.

The year is still young
when you are here my one love
green will always show

It was the second poem she'd found on her desk. The first hadn't been very good. This was alright, but not amazing.

She knew who it was from. The young one in the jeans. She wanted to go over and tell him. The year is still young because it's April, it has nothing to do with me. She wanted to thank him for putting his verses in envelopes so that no one else knew

117

they were there and to ask if perhaps from now on he could just leave the envelopes and dispense with the poetry. Envelopes were useful, after all.

He circled towards her desk and she typed.

He sat and wheeled himself towards her in an office chair and she typed.

'Could I just interrupt a minute?'

She glanced up and checked the collar of his shirt. It wasn't new, but it was clean and perfectly smooth. Not a goblin.

'Of course you can. What is it?'

'I wondered what you thought of the poems. I know you read poetry, I've seen you do it. I mean, I like the photography and it just about earns me a living, but I want to write. It's difficult finding someone you can show things to.'

'Embarrassing.'

'I thought you'd understand.'

'Well, we should talk about it sometime. Come round and have tea. Would that be nice?'

Tea was nice and motherly, it wouldn't scare him. Apparently, he needed not to be scared. 'I wondered what you thought of the poems.' Was that serious? What should she tell him? You may not be a goblin, but your poetry is dreadful and your chat-up lines are worse?

Besides which, who would send you anonymous poems on love and then explain they were only literature? He didn't seem to notice that was insulting.

She continued with her typing. When she was into the flow of it, the words lined across the paper, as if she was rubbing the whiteness away; not putting a blackness on. She was squeezing the words out from where they were already hiding. That was a comfortable idea. It had nothing to do with the sense of what she wrote, nothing to do with reality at all and it meant that she couldn't be wrong, because she was only finding something, not inventing it. She didn't know if she wanted the feeling this gave her, but it stopped her from making spelling mistakes.

The tea was planned for Sunday, which made it Sunday Tea. She bought an oily cherry cake and a tea pot. She hadn't bothered with a pot, just for herself.

The flat the young man arrived at was still quite new to her. In a red sandstone tenement, with solid walls, it had suited her before she moved in and now it suited her more. The rent was high, but she was managing. When he stepped into the hall, across one of her new rugs, he was obviously impressed. Surprised.

'You do read a lot, don't you?'

The hall was lined with cheap bookshelves, all filled. She was proud of them all.

'I might just like the way they fill the space. I might not have read even one.' She smiled and led him into the living room, made him sit down.

She had already decided how the afternoon would go. It wouldn't.

Sending her poems like that. He annoyed her in the same way the office annoyed her. Both of them imagined they were outside reality. She always enjoyed her stories and fairy tales, but she didn't want them all the time. It felt like living with the Goblins - it stifled her breath.

'So, about your poems, Ben. If I can call you Ben.'

'Sure, sure. I'm sorry, nobody seems to call you by your name. I don't know it.'

'Nobody knows it. It's a private thing.'

'Oh.'

'You must have read the old stories. If you give someone your name, you're giving them power over you. It's funny how few people notice.'

'Yes.'

'Who are you writing to? In the poems. Who are they to?'

'No one. No one in particular. I thought that would be better. Whoever read them could think it was someone they knew. Anyone. A woman. A man.' 'A parrot.'

'What?'

'I mean, they feel anonymous. They're very warm, but they're very anonymous.'

'I see.'

'They'll probably do very well.'

'I'm sorry?'

'Look over there, in the corner. You gave me the idea. For want of a better description, they're tie-dyed pyjamas and little hats.'

'Whose are they.'

'I don't know yet. I make them and sell them. I do quite well. The first ones, I gave to the students who stayed in my old place. I vary the design and the cloth is always different. Sometimes I prepare it, sometimes art students. To be accurate, it's printing, not tie-dye.'

'Wonderful. I never knew.'

'It's not wonderful. It's rubbish. They sell for four or five times what they cost to make; they fit no one; they're garish and poorly sewn. We live in a cold, wet city and these are as thin as handkerchiefs and just about as warm; they're criminal. But I can sell them and I can make money. They're anonymous, too, so they sell.'

'I ran away from my husband and now I make clothes by a river. I even put a little label inside them: "Cap O'Rushes", do you see? Like the woman in the story.'

'Yes, I remember it.'

'I thought you would. Ask anyone in that office and probably they would - it would be their style. Ask them what was in the paper yesterday and they wouldn't have a clue. Beggars and wizards and wise old men: we have beggars now, do they know that?'

'Of course, you can't avoid them.'

'Yes, you can. If you couldn't avoid them, they wouldn't still be there.'

'Cap O'Rushes went back to her husband - will you do that?'

'What do you think?'

'I don't think you'll stick to the plot.'

'Well no, neither do I. '

'But I should stick to photographs, right?'

'It isn't up to me. You should maybe write stories, or plays, or maybe your poems are terrific and I wasn't the right person to ask.'

'I thought you didn't like stories.'

'I do like some. But they're only by dead people - you couldn't compete. '

For the rest of the afternoon, they talked like human beings. She refreshed the tea pot and told him her name. Being careful was one thing, but sometimes, she could border on the eccentric. She was sad when he had to go, but a little relieved, so he must have left at about the right time.

When the evening began to darken, she drew the curtains and sat back in the corner of the sofa, her shoes off and her feet curled underneath her. She was so relaxed. She had been all day. If she had a good, female friend she could have told her how relaxing it was for an apparently single woman to finally know that she didn't have to care. They would have laughed and then been serious about that. There was no need to lean on an absent boyfriend, or a husband. People could think she was gay, or frigid, or mad, or whatever they wanted, it didn't matter. She was enough in herself, which made her confident, which made her enough in herself. That was very good. A real strength.

She wished it hadn't taken her so many years to be strong.

It was odd that Ben had asked her if she would go back to Colin and the boys. In the story, she should have waited, for example, five years, because that was her lucky number and then she would have gone back in disguise.

Fuck that.

If she did ever run into Colin, she would tell him that she did still love him as much as she could. And now she knew how much she could. She had stretched and grown into work and business, happiness and her own home. She knew who she was and that she was capable of as much as wanted to be. That was very nice.

The thing about Colin was that she still only loved as much as she could. And that still wasn't very much at all.

It wasn't her fault. No one can ever do more than what they can. It wasn't because he was a goblin, either; she wouldn't need to tell him stories about that. She simply couldn't find him lovable. That was the truth and that was all.

She felt, now, she was finished with all that.

The seaside photographer

I came to the library and I don't know why.

There's an old man behind me and he's breathing like a big cat in a cage. It's a loud, fierce breath that should come with running, with pulling back at the anger before you fight, with making love. This man is blue round his lips and gasping from sitting in a chair and reading the morning's paper.

I came to be in the library and I don't know why. The air is full of reading and now you can't read and I didn't think of that before I got here. I just came to the library, not knowing why.

This was a good day. The umbrella has stayed in my bag, telescoped and rolled up tight. Dawn started slowly. And I was up to see it rise; the milky blue dawn, clear and almost chill, that brought in a hot, sweet afternoon. It is now a very gentle evening and, if I could see them, the clouds would be blushing or burning, or sculling off with the sun, towards the west. Whichever would be the most appropriate.

When I don't have a book of my own, I read Ed McBain. Whatever they have with his name on I read until it's time for me to leave and each of the unfinished pieces has collided and combined. There are severed heads in airline holdalls and burnt up bodies tied with wire. When I read them, I liked the characters and the way he talks about Spring, but afterwards, it's the pathology that clings. There'll be a reason for that, but I don't know it.

Twice I've ever seen you with a book. The first one you set on the windowsill as soon as I came into the sitting room, because you always preferred to talk. That was a Western with a desert coloured cover and its price in pence and shillings on the front. You gave me the second one later, when I couldn't get to sleep. It was an Alistair MacLean, I think, quite new. I didn't like it and I still couldn't sleep.

You keep watch in the night, you always have. I remember your coughs and the creaking, you slipping into the toilet to have a smoke and shadowing out to the back to look at the night. I knew. I heard you. You never slept. McBain might not have suited you, might not have been just right, but I wish I had given you something then, to save you from the dark.

For me it happened today, this good day. I woke, having dreamed a little, and washed and spent hours full of the small things to do with me. I worked. Also, I answered the telephone. It told me how different your day had been. This day and how many before it.

I wanted to call you and say things, or say nothing and hope that you would know.

I don't understand what I should do.

I have you in my head and it's all lies. Not memories, lies. You are walking through the snowy zoo with your black umbrella, striding with it furled, wanting to show me the bears, or the parrots. I am in the shadow of your overcoat, my hand in the pocket of your overcoat, down among the tickle of cellophane and peppermints and I am warm. It feels like Good King Wenceslas and I'm wishing for a blizzard to come, to let me step in your footprints and still be warm. Later, at the bus stop, I can wrap both my arms around one of yours and let it lift me up. I can swing.

But this leads me to other places now, to a path between woods, under sugar loaf cones of orange lamplight and warm rain where I walked with my fingers laced in other fingers and our hands in the pocket of his rain coat while he talked. It was the last night we could have before he went away. My third

123

time ever and every time with him.

Each of these things makes the other one a lie. There is nothing to keep them apart, these lies, year, on year, on year, and each one becomes another. Except that I see his face as I can see it today and your face is fifteen years out of date. You are not in my dreams, as he is, but I love you both.

When I was young I thought you had everything you wanted. You'll remember once, I asked if you were rich. It wasn't out of greed, not even curiosity, I was sure in my heart that you were a millionaire. I just wanted the thrill of hearing you say it out loud. I would have kept it to myself. I didn't know that you would always give, whether you were able to or not. I didn't know what you did when I wasn't there. To me, you could not have been anything but happy and certain and wanting to give, because you were made like that.

A while ago I watched another man turn to walk away on a summer street and if he had been a child of mine, straying too near to the kerb, not quite safe, I would have felt the same. Just for a moment I wanted to call him back. The way you always want to call them back, to say something, anything. To wish them well, although they won't understand it if you do. You would have watched me like that, without my understanding. You were only the same as everyone else. Not rich, not always happy, not always certain, not born to be safe. And you had no power.

I realised that sooner and younger than anything else and you know that I blamed you. I thought you had made a decision to be weak, that you could make that decision, and that it was your fault. When you said they should call off all the wars and work it out with the gloves on, up in the ring, it was you that I saw. Your hair in a glossy black crew cut, with the flag a discreet block of colour on the shine of your white vest, high boots and long shorts, the saviour of your nation. Of course, you hadn't fought for years; not since before I was born, but you still had the build and the faith in your muscle. I believed in your faith.

I stood next to you in your kitchen and leaned the way you were leaning, over the window, over the edge. I made it so that our shoulders were touching and feeling the warmth through your shirt made me shiver as we looked out the back. Through the window it was icy mist and your cigarette threaded out to join it and there was dead quiet out there, like the ghost of a dawn.

My mouth was still tasteless with sleep and my eyes kept yawning back and trying to close and you said to me,

I thought you were going to stay longer,

and kept on looking out. I couldn't think of any words.

So my father led me away, past the bed that we would have made later and that would have been still warm from where I'd slept. I knew that you weren't going to stop him, that's why I never asked. I never even cried.

You couldn't stop your daughter's husband, like you couldn't stop the wars.

I'm sorry. I don't think as sorry as you.

The things that made you, I'll never see. You told me all about London before the war, when you were the champion of the works; the Black Country apprentice, taking all comers on. There was the time when the man got caught in the overhead belts and went up and round and was dead before they got him down. You didn't talk much about it, but I remember. Every one else had gone to bed and I was up late, listening, when you said about the white hot bar and the way it just touched the chest of this one man and went straight on through. You looked at his back and saw daylight before he fell.

After that you stopped yourself in case you gave me dreams. You didn't. I felt the same way that I did when you took me down to your work. A Sunday, no one else there and, I don't know how, but you let us in and the whole place was as if it belonged to you. Every one of those machines you understood, and you could set all that heaviness in motion at a touch. You could conjure up whirling and screaming that filled the shop and set strange new components slithering out, still hot. You pattered me along the corridors left between the machines and all of it was waiting for the switch to set up a roar, with the bitter smell of sweat and metal stirred up everywhere we stepped.

Just for the afternoon you were the master and the owner and the magician for me. We kept that our secret afterwards.

I don't know what made you how you are. I wasn't there on

the day you decided there were changes you could no longer make and now you would stay with turn-ups, stay with flannel for underwear and after Heath, you would stop voting and each year would put you closer to your past.

Now there is a change for the worst. I don't understand how these things happen. Perhaps you took too many punches and they hurt inside your head, perhaps the little sparks of iron that caught you were finally too much, or perhaps it was always being patient, only letting the pressure show with the tap and tap and tap from your nervous foot in the dark of the room. All these cancers you collect through time; they are in you but not of you and yet part of what people think of, whenever they think of you. They are as real as you. Each one of them could be a reason, it could be none of them, it could be all. Whatever the cause you are blind now. Suddenly.

I have no magic for you and there is nothing I have learned to make. If, in this world, I could, I would write you whole and well. I would write you smiling through windy sunshine and strolling with your wife, the thin boards of the promenade beneath you, reaching up to a seaside photographer. I would wish myself unborn and you as you were in a holiday picture. A picture I have lost.

As it is, you are more and better now than ever you were then, a more beautiful and perfect, breathing man. Nothing should dare touch you, not a thing. Only, the years and the years' hardness, they were out and waiting for you from the start.

All I can do is write you words you cannot read and feel them between us.

The Last

On the seventh day of mourning for a dead Iranian priest and the seventh day since bicycles and bodies filled a Chinese square, she walked towards home as dawn overtook the city. As one body became a legend and a pilgrimage and how many thousand others vanished in enforced forgetfulness, she crossed an empty road to wait by the hamburger van for a roll and bacon. She was hungry, suddenly.

The taste of hot salt and floury bread was still in her mouth as she came to the close and climbed the stair. She was starting to feel dizzy; lack of sleep, she supposed, and stopped on one of the landings to look out and take a breath. A misty sunrise was staring to catch the rooftops. It flared across a sheen of old rain and snuffed out the last of the street lamps as the world turned into light. Today it would be hot again.

Stale heat met her when she unlocked the door and the rooms were caught in yesterday, somehow, silent inside drawn curtains. She undressed in the bathroom and washed, enjoying the feel of water, only slightly thicker than the air and cool.

Through in the bedroom she brushed and brushed her hair, let her shoulders relax and let the smell of another house fall around her. The smell of another bedroom, another bed, in what had become another home. She thought how strange it was; the times you missed people. Just before you saw them

127

again and just after they were gone. Or you were gone.

Now she must get to her bed. It was waiting there, in the corner, with its thin, summer coverlet and its ghosts.

All beds have ghosts. They play host to deaths, conceptions, births and indiscretions. They support us in our dreams and in our nightmares and they remember things. Overlooking our armchairs and cupboards, we fill our beds with inadvertent haunting. This was a young bed, as beds go, and had only two ghosts.

She padded across from the mirror, the heat of the room against her skin like cloth, and let herself in between the sheets. She lay on the left hand side of the bed, the side that was furthest from the wall.

There now.

She stared at the dark she kept behind her eyelids. It was never just plain black. If you looked, there was a pattern of colours that mingled and scattered round a moving centre. The centre was sometimes a colour and sometimes a space. With one bird singing at the back of the house, she peered ahead. Her mother would have said she was looking at nothing: she would have said it was only a thing which she didn't understand, but then, she had always preferred the view when her eyes were shut.

So glad you could spare the time to come home.
Mm hm.

The dark, wee voice slipped inside her head, just a little louder than a breath.

I'm amazed that someone can manage with so little sleep. And you're lying on me. Again
How can I be lying on you? You're not there.
Then how come you're talking to me? Eh?

To be honest, it wasn't the same as her husband's voice. Oh, she recognised it, certainly, it couldn't be anyone else, but it wasn't quite him, all the same. Bobby hadn't been so clever, or so hard. Now he would appear; a thin, wiry sound, like a mosquito in the night, perhaps outside the window and per-

128

haps beside your ear. You couldn't quite tell where he was. Bobby was an irritation.

You're lying on me. This is my side.

Which was true, Bobby had always slept on the left hand side. It belonged to him. He was there to be clambered over, or crawled around. For eleven years she had been sandwiched between his back and the wall, his stomach and the wall, his elbows and his knees and the wall. After she and the bed had left him, she hadn't felt safe at night for months. She would tug pillows under the covers and sleep with their slightly prickly pressure at her back. She enjoyed her space now, dreamed expansively, and was glad she hadn't weakened and bought a single bed.

You should have bought a single bed; you're a single woman.

Of course, the old bed had its drawbacks.

Go away, Bobby, I want to sleep.

You telling me you're not single? You're not married, you're not engaged, you must be single. Or has he proposed? Has he asked you, hen? Is that what he's done? That's nice.

He hasn't proposed. Don't be stupid.

Aw, the bad bugger. Never mind, well, perhaps he will. There's still time. Just about.

I can turn you off, you know, if I want to.

You always did.

That isn't true.

Hffff.

If I stop thinking about you you will disappear.

On you go, then.

She know that you can't not think of something. It's impossible. In order not to think of it, you have to think of it, so that you know what it is you're not thinking of. Only then you are thinking of it, so you have to start again. In the last few months, since Bobby's little chats had started, she had been kept awake until dawn with games like this. She would concentrate and concentrate until there seemed to be no sign of him. She might even begin to doze and then, there would be Bobby, darting in again. He was hard to get rid of. Crafty.

Hey. Have you made me disappear, yet? I can't tell?
The only thing to do was to picture the real Bobby and where he must be, right now. She put him in a bed, a new single bed, in the bedroom they once shared. She closed his eyes and made him asleep. He was across the river in another place where she didn't see him and she didn't have to care. She folded up the idea of him and threw it away.

Now, she would lie and try to sleep and, if it didn't work, she could always find a book to read. She had lots of books since Bobby. Poetry and politics and the people that you ought to read, like Hardy, even if all she remembered of him was how filthy the weather was. For enjoyment, she chose science fiction, any kind. Philip K. Dick and Asimov, Richard McKenna. They were always so comfortable. They wrote about whole worlds, as if they were only a town or two, maybe a wee continent. And if the whole world ended, there was something afterwards. Something left.

The glow through her curtains was bright now, the sun fully up. She turned on her side and pulled the sheet across her eyes. The dark became darker. Maybe it was time for a pillow again. Not that it would be filling Bobby's space. Not this time. It would be pulled down beside her to press against her stomach and be held and it would fill a new space.

Martin: six inches taller, twelve years younger, shorter hair and longer fingers, made out of different bones and different skin. Martin.

They were different people. Their voices were not the same and nor was their laughter. This separation of bodies, this certain privacy, had always seemed a natural thing between people before. With Martin, it became a source of pain.

She had walked home past the darkened shops, televisions broadcasting greyness, empty fishmongers' windows and butchers' slabs and she had wanted to go back to him. She had wanted to be with him; to be him. Skin against skin wasn't close enough. She wanted to touch him from the inside out and to let him do as much with her. Even her teeth ached for him.

Daft.

And they hadn't started well. It hadn't begun as she intended.

There she had been, inches away from leaving Bobby and needing to be unfaithful to him. Then there would be no doubt, no going back, she would have made her decision. And Martin was it. She had intended to use him, which wasn't good.

Martin had been very nice to her, flirted a wee bit, and it hadn't taken much to get him to invite her over for a meal and they both knew what that could mean, if they wanted. It hadn't seemed destined to last.

Bobby was informed she would be gone for two days on a trip, as part of her college course. College was like school and weans at school took trips, so that was fine by him. He didn't even ask where she was going. She told him in any case. The Bulb Fields. She had a friend who'd been there.

Twelve hours before her dinner with Martin, she took a taxi to a Bed and Breakfast place in a part of the town she hardly knew. It was almost like a real holiday. She lay on her bed and watched the little portable TV, then had lunch at a tea shop that she found. Then she came back, dozed, showered and took a long time getting dressed.

Everything was new, at least everything that counts. Knickers, bra, stockings, suspenders, the full, traditional kit for such occasions, all matching, crisp and new. They smelt good. From Marks and Spencer. She didn't like their clothes, especially not when Margaret Thatcher said she wore them, it seemed to make them partisan, but their underwear was good, a good fit. According to Steve at the college, they made men's stuff just as well. That was the kind of thing Steve would say. Catch Bobby discussing his underpants with a woman.

Martin had told her eight o'clock would be fine and she set out from the guest house at just on the hour, so that she could apologise for being that slightest bit late. She had to take another taxi, but it was worth it. When he opened the door, he would see what she intended him to see: nothing ruffled, her makeup right, relaxed, but self-possessed.

It took a while for him to come to the door, so long, she thought she must have the wrong address. But then there were footsteps, a cough and the sound of unlocking.

You're early.

Not really. I think I'm a wee bit late.

Late? Oh, I'm sorry, Kath.

Why? What's the matter? Shall I come back later on?

No. No. I really apologise There's nothing wrong except my brain. Come in. Come in. Please, come in.

He looked hot. He looked dirty. He smelled of sweat. His hands, arms, trainers, jeans and T-shirt were dotted and smeared with paint. Kath wondered if it was all some kind of joke.

She was led along a hallway covered in sheets of newspaper and piles of ornaments and Martin showed her into a kitchen where nothing was being cooked.

Kath had intended to leave. She would have a cup of coffee and say that he was obviously busy. Perhaps they could set a date for some other time. When the other time would be, she would leave indefinite. But, when he had turned on the kettle and come to sit beside her at the kitchen table, he took her head between his hands and apologised. He hadn't forgotten her, only what time it was. As soon as you painted one room, you needed to paint them all; they looked so shabby in comparison. She knew how it was. Then he kissed her on the cheek and asked her what he should wear for her.

He was sincere. His hair was thinning slightly, over the crown and his breath smelt a little stale. And he was sincere. She almost left again, because she had intended to use him. His sincerity rubbed off. She smiled.

Do you have a suit?

I do, if you insist.

I insist.

In her bed the other ghost was waking; the one she kept with her now. As she lay on her side, it formed along her back; the shape and pressure of Martin. His memory in her skin. There was the touch of his stomach against her spine, there was his arm, reaching over, there was his breath in her hair, hot and cold and hot. There he was. However she turned, the feel of him would be on her until she slept and sometimes then, too.

132

If I'm going to wear the suit, I'll have to shave and stuff. Do you mind sitting about on your own for a bit?

No.

Well, you have your coffee and I'll have mine when I'm ready. Is there anything else you want?

I don't think so.

Fine. Do tell me if there is.

He smiled a big, broad smile and went out to lather soap and run taps. She listened to the sounds she might hear any morning, if she'd stayed the night. For a moment or two, he appeared in the doorway, wearing a dressing gown and still smiling.

I couldn't just stay like this?

No.

Too distracting for you?

Too cold. For you.

Come and give us a kiss, then. Please.

And she did walk over and come close enough to kiss. Martin didn't try to hold her, but when she had brushed his cheek with her lips, he used his thumb and forefinger to gently close her eyes. She heard the movement of cloth and then felt his free hand slide around her and pull her in. She held him, her hands inside his dressing gown, against his skin, her cheek against his neck. He was very warm. The aftershave was fresh on his hands and face and there was the smell of heat and him. He only let Kath open her eyes when they were standing apart and he was all wrapped up again. Neither of them said a word.

Wearing the suit, Martin ordered them two pizzas, which duly arrived, and when Kath only picked at hers, he ate it, too. She knew she would remember the next bit, because it was one of those times that feel significant. She could feel herself watching herself, as she took his hand and kissed it, feeling it wasn't right because she shouldn't make the moves. It wasn't her place. It might be the place of other women; just not her. He stopped talking and looked at her.

I'm very tired, Kath. Really tired. I'm working all kinds of hours and doing college too and it's driving me mad. And all this painting. I mean, I want to go to bed. Now. Would you like to come too?

She nodded, looking him straight in the eye, which sur-

133

prised her.

Will you come to bed with me, Kath? Will you sleep with me? Will you like that? Will you take all your clothes off and be next to me with all my clothes off in the same bed? Will you do that? Will you be in bed with me, naked, all night? All night, Kath? Will you be there when I wake up? Will you come to bed? Will you? My bed? Mmh? Go on.

She remembered the next bit, too. She remembered nearly laughing.

Martin was in bed already and lying still when she walked into his bedroom in the dark, with all of that underwear wasted, off before he could see it. She was careful not to stub her toes on the piles of books and he lifted the covers politely for her to climb in. There was the introductory clumsiness as they tried out a first embrace. He kissed her face, slowly: eyes, mouth, forehead, ears, mouth, cheeks, and then they pulled themselves into a tighter hug. He felt friendly. Then his arms seemed to give a little and he fell asleep.

It was ridiculous. Kath stared into the shapes and shadows of the room with Martin's weight beginning to numb her arm. His breathing faded into a soft, comfortable rhythm and he was gone for the night. Tonight, they would sleep together. Just that: they would be together and asleep. Kath wondered why she wasn't disappointed and then giggled.

Through the city some were waking and some were walking into the places where they felt they could talk to God. Kath was almost asleep. The sun was high and strong already, almost too hot, and, after lunch, the space between houses would be filled with still bodies, children and portable barbecues. Cats would lie along window sills and walls, too intent upon the excess of heat to purr. Elsewhere, polar bears would drown in melting ice fields and farmers would wake and be surprised by dust, a plague of dust.

Bobby said she'd caught the sun, when she got back. She hadn't. Still, there was something about facing him again that made her expect him to notice a change. It was like standing in front of her father, the morning after a boy named White had put his hand right up her skirt. She'd felt sure that the shape of her face must have changed. That something of the change inside her would show.

Bobby was not her father and she was no longer seventeen, but it wouldn't be too remarkable if the light in her eyes was sharper, or brighter, or there was something new about her smile.

Kath thought it better to say that, yes, she had caught the sun, and let that be the reason for any change. Bobby said she looked nice with a bit of colour and didn't want to know about the bulbs. Kath didn't tell him. Not about Martin and not about the bulbs.

For the next few weeks she got used to being herself. Inside her house, inside her clothes, and inside that, there she was with her secret: the one that made her laugh when there was no one else to see. She had gone to bed with a man and done nothing at all but sleep and sleep contentedly. The following day, while her husband thought she was looking at daffodils, she stayed in Martin's bed while he went off to the guest house to pick up her case. He said he was her cousin and, the night before, she'd been suddenly taken sick. He settled the bill and came straight home with wishes for her speedy recovery. Before he went away they made love and when he got back, they fucked and then made love. They spent the day watching television and eating sandwiches and from time to time, they would jump on each other again. Then they declared dusk early and went to bed. She didn't think that either of them even mentioned bulbs.

You'll go to Hell.

After you.

No, hen, this is serious. Burny, burny. You'll die and you will go to Hell. You'll burn.

People don't go to Hell for being happy.

Depends what makes you happy, doesn't it? Murder, adultery...

I don't believe in any of that, Bobby.

Aye, but it scares you, though.

Dying scares me, that's all. It scares me to think of being dead.

Scares me too, hen. It scares me too, See you around then.

Bye.

Martin's ghost never talked to her; it was only something that she felt. Kath tried to feel it now, to get it back beside her, but Martin faded in the way he always did at the slightest sign of guilt. Somewhere, somebody set off a car alarm and it squealed into the morning, jerking her more awake. She would have to distract herself and consider other things for a while, or else she would imagine being buried, imagine being nothing at all.

She thought of the bus driver yesterday who'd jumped from his cab with his regulation dark green trousers, rolled up to his knees, It was this heat, it got to everyone.

Then there was the young girl with the close cropped hair who had sat on the other side of the bus, dressed entirely in black. Canvas shoes, long johns, T-shirt and a sagging mohair sweater, all black. She must have been so hot and yet she hadn't looked it.

Kath wondered why black mohair sweaters always seemed to be shapeless. She wondered if people bought them specially with tunnel sleeves and gaping necks and rat's tails of loose wool. You never seemed to see them in the shops.

Then Kath thought about the heat.

It wouldn't have worried her before. She would maybe have noticed that the birds were dying; dark birds in particular. Ravens, crows, jackdaws, blackbirds. More and more she was passing them on verges, or in gutters, lying still and perfect, as if they were dozing. This must have something to do with the heat, she was sure of that, but all she would have noticed before was the brown grass, the dead birds and the constant awareness of sweat.

Now she was in the habit of thinking, of trying to understand. Kath looked in magazines for articles on the Greenhouse Effect. She was aware that, on Madeira, the gadfly petrel's eggs were being eaten by introduced rats and soon there would be no more petrels and no more of their lonely hooting by the cliffs.

She also knew there were poisons in food and drink; in earth, air and water. She knew of the variety of slow, invisible deaths and that perhaps, even now, she was dying from one thing or another. Perhaps from the heat.

It wasn't the best time to start to be aware of things. It wasn't the best time to recognise the names of politicians, or what they did. If she was seventeen she would only be thinking of Martin; there wouldn't be room for anything else. But she was forty-two and finding it hard whenever she tried to lose weight. She wasn't grey, but she would be and it wouldn't be long coming. Martin was lovely, but alone in her bed, she thought about God and dying more than him. That was how everything ended, after all. Sometimes things could feel very pointless.

That evening, yesterday evening, now, they really did have dinner at his flat. She bought him what she wanted and she cooked it, which seemed to be quite an acceptable deal for a man of his generation. Or perhaps he was just more reasonable than most. They ate late and listened to a play on the radio while they did it. No candles, but a bottle of wine and then another and then lying on the floor in the sitting room with a cushion from the sofa under their heads. They watched a film about a mad plastic surgeon, together in the dark and went to bed before the one about the comet that was heading straight for Earth.

Stomach against stomach, they talked softly, seriously. They decided against children. It was sad, but Kath was getting a bit too old to think about it, really. Not that they didn't want them, wouldn't like them, it just didn't seem appropriate. They hadn't talked about it before and it gave them a strange feeling to agree this wasn't a world for children. Martin kissed her and they held each other tighter for a while and didn't talk.

Normally she stayed the night, if they went to bed. No point in staying there all that time, even getting drowsy, and then going to sleep somewhere else. Not to mention how good it was to wake up with company, sometimes, to wake up before him and see his face asleep. Anyone would fancy him asleep. She was glad he didn't do it in public.

This time, she couldn't sleep, couldn't settle, and so she went home. More because she needed a walk than anything else. Martin had understood. She'd let him lie in and call him later, to make sure.

She would probably ask him over, too, because she'd been looking at houses in the papers and they should be thinking of

137

buying now. You couldn't live together in two different houses. They should talk about it all. What they should do.

Kath wanted to live with him. They should have one home between them and make it the way that suited them, sharing the work. Martin could paint it. She didn't think they would marry, but they would certainly settle down. Kath found it very difficult to put into words, but she felt their time was somehow limited. It was important. You only ever had the length of your life to get things done and she supposed you should hurry, anyway, and not settle for second best, but perhaps it would be sensible to hurry even more than usual and to arrange the things you wanted now.

The century was ending, which meant nothing, but it felt significant. It worried her. It was another thing that worried her. Tonight she would tell Martin that their affairs should be set in order and made right. Just in case. Imagine if they were the last on Earth, say they were to be the sole survivors, what would they do? It was only a game, a state of mind to be in, she knew that. Still, it seemed to be the best way they could live; taking each day; being alive through each day; making the most of their joy.

Kath felt herself sink into sleep; aware of losing awareness and liking it. Next, she would sleep, while dawn rolled round the world towards tomorrow. Today it was hot.